# DRAGON TALES

### Book VI

## The Dragons'
## Call

For Ben and
Emma
with love.

Judy

XX

This is the sixth of the Dragon Tales Chronicles.
Already published:
*Dragon Tales Book I: Quest for a Cave*
*Dragon Tales Book II: Quest for a Friend*
*Dragon Tales Book III: Quest for Adventure*
*Dragon Tales Book IV: The Runaway*
*Dragon Tales Book V: Dragons in Snow*
*The Dragon Tales Colouring Book*

# DRAGON TALES

## BOOK VI

# The Dragons' Call

by

**Judy Hayman**

illustrated by

**Caroline Wolfe Murray**

Practical Inspiration
PUBLISHING

First published in Great Britain by Practical
Inspiration Publishing, 2016

ISBN (print): 978-1-910056-48-6
ISBN (ebook): 978-1-910056-49-3

For more information on the Dragon Tales books,
email info@alisonjones.com.

This last one is for Peter, with love and gratitude.
And for Alison, whose Sunday dinner debt is repaid
many times over.
J.L.H.


For the children of Saltoun Primary School.
C.W.M.

# What young readers say about the Dragon Tales books

'I like that the dragons go on adventures and have so much fun, and I love Ben McIlwhinnie. Emily's my favourite dragon because she loves books like I do.' - *Catherine, Basingstoke*

'Thank you for the dragon books. My favourite is *Quest for a Friend* because I find Desmond really entertaining, and I think the baby is really cool.' - *Jessica, Guildford, Surrey*

'I love the Bonxie bird in *Quest for Adventure*. He is really funny. I love his Scottish words and really laughed when he was telling the other birds to leave Des alone in Ice Land, especially when he told them not to poo on Des.' - *Kirstyn, Clackmannanshire*

'I like Tom because he is really funny. I am reading Book 4 and enjoying the dragons trying to find Ollie and flying to different places.' - *Fraser, Southall, Notts*

'I love how the books get more and more exciting. Also I like the way the books are worded. I like the way the dragons show their feelings because they are like people. My favourite is Des, because he takes all sorts of risks.' - *Aly, Haddington, East Lothian*

My favourite character is Tom, and I liked the bit where he did a head-stand in the water, and how he sits on Ben McIlwhinnie's ear. - *Matthew, Staveley, Derbyshire*

'I love the way that all of the dragons in *Quest for a Cave* are shades of blue. And it is funny when Emily thought the JCB digger was a yellow dragon! - *Jarosan, Yateley, Hants*

'Magical, increasing and believing the unbelievable, all describes the Dragon Chronicles. Good for a large age range. - ' *Zara, Fleet, Hants*

'*Quest for a Cave* was a fun childhood read with an interesting twist. I am looking forward to the next books.' 'Very enjoyable! I liked the mountain giant best.' - *Kayla and Ailsa, Musselburgh, East Lothian*

'I really enjoyed *Dragon Tales* because I felt like I was there. I like drawing pictures of Tom playing on the mountain giant's ear.' - *Skye, Edinburgh*

'Our favourite character is Lily, because she is a baby dragon with a lot of temper. She is the classic bossy little sister!' - *Stella and Sarah, Haydon Bridge, Northumberland*

'I love these books because it's very exciting to read about dragon families and their adventures. I can't wait to read more.' - *Molly, Glasgow*

'We liked the part in Book 4 where Georgie pulled Tom's spiky tail because he wanted to play.' - *Lucy and Andrew, Edinburgh*

'I've read all the books and I really enjoyed them. I liked the dragon tail sign on each chapter.' - *Haruka, Japan*

'I like dragons, so I really like all your books. My sisters Skyla and Milly loved hearing what dragons like to eat and looking at Elise's pictures. My favourite book is *The Runaway*, because Ollie ends up getting found by people and now they are looking for all the dragons. It makes it exciting to keep reading - *Kaleb, New Zealand*

# Table of Contents

## Chapter 1

# Spring on the Way

A loud yell from Tom made everybody jump. Emily, Alice and Ollie, who had been looking out of the other three windows of the Tower room in Aunt Angelica's Castle, looked round startled. Des, sorting his travelling bundle in the middle of his untidy hay bed, even leapt to his feet. Then they all began to laugh. Tom had leaned too far out of his window and a huge dollop of melting snow had fallen from the roof onto his head, covering one eye and lodging itself onto his bright blue spikes.

"Idiot!" said Ollie.

"Don't shake your head!" said Emily, but was too late. A vigorous shake from Tom sent drips of wet snow flying across the room. Des growled as the largest dollop landed on his bed.

"Why are you lot lurking up here anyway?" he complained. "We know the snow's melting at last. There's no need to watch it happen!" He gave a suspicious glare round the four young dragons. "I don't suppose you're watching out for those little Human friends of yours, are you?"

Emily and Alice assumed expressions of innocence, but Ollie scowled. "They're no friends of mine!" he declared.

"Huh, you like playing with that ball they gave you as much as Tom does," Alice said, making Ollie scowl even more. "And we're NOT looking for them, Des. There's been no sign of them. They promised to leave us alone, and they *have* done. You're far too suspicious. Typical grown-up! Come on, Emily – let's go out."

She flounced out of the room with her nose in the air and Emily followed, flashing Des an apologetic glance as she went. Tom tried to stay behind, but a determined shove from Ollie sent him out after the girls, and the battered door was firmly shut behind him. He sighed and trailed slowly down the stairs as

Alice and Emily squeezed through the hole in the front door, and disappeared into the garden.

He headed for the kitchen. Maggie might feel sorry for him left on his own, and find him a snack.

Out in the garden, Emily and Alice headed for their favourite place. It was a flat branch growing sideways out of the trunk of an ash tree at the edge of the garden. The trees of the wood grew thickly behind it on the other side of the boundary fence, so there was little chance of being spotted from outside. Fortunately they were mainly fir trees, so even in winter the dragons were well hidden. They flew up, settled side by side facing the Castle and hoped that nobody would disturb them.

"When the leaves come out we'll be completely hidden up here," said Alice.

Emily looked at her, puzzled. "We won't be here then," she said. "Dad's wing is nearly better. As soon as the snow's completely gone, and he's strong enough, we'll be heading home to our cave. And you're coming too, aren't you?"

"I hope so," said Alice. "But it will depend on what the parents decide. I think they quite like living here, even with old Ange. It's better for Grandad." She sighed heavily, and Emily decided to change the subject.

"I *was* looking out for Lisa and the others," she admitted. "I know we said we wouldn't, but I'd LOVE to see them again, wouldn't you?"

The young dragons had had a fright a few weeks previously, at the height of the snowy winter, when four Human children had discovered their secret hide-out in the old ruined house that was Alice's Aunt Angelica's home. The winter had been so severe that she had invited all her family to join her in her 'castle', and had taken in Emily's family too, when their cave had been blocked with snow. There was plenty of room for them all, but Emily knew that as soon as her father's broken wing had healed, he would want to return home to their cave in the Scottish glen. And she wanted to go home herself – but she wanted her friends to come too!

"I knew they'd keep their promise," Alice said. "There's been no sign of any other Human in the woods, so they can't have told anybody else about us. And Des blocked up the hole in the fence, so they couldn't get back in, even if they sneaked back this way themselves. I'm glad the parents never found out, though."

"It was nice of them to give us those books," Emily said. "I wish I could have said thank you!" She twiddled the coloured bobble on her arm, looked at the blue one that Alice wore, the token of friendship that Lisa had given them, and decided to confess. "I'd love to sneak out and get a proper look at the place they live in! Wouldn't you?"

Alice, who was a little older and a good deal more sensible, looked at her severely. "Don't even DREAM about it!" she said. "Forget them. It was great, but it's finished. We were lucky only Des found out. Stop talking about them." Looking at the scowl on Emily's face she added hastily. "It's chilly out here. Let's see if it's supper time."

They flew down from the branch and across to the front door, over patches of bright green that were appearing as the snow gradually melted. There were still deep drifts in many places, and the clouds were low in the sky, threatening rain. Winter was departing, but the outside world was not inviting, and the young dragons were still confined to the tangled garden of the old house, inside the high fence. Sighing for the summer and the wide open spaces of her beloved Scottish glen, Emily followed Alice inside.

Meanwhile, up in the Tower room, Ollie had taken advantage of having Des to himself, and was using his most persuasive tactics. The sight of the battered travelling gear had made him realise that it would not be long before Des's itchy wings got the better of him, and he set off on his travels again. As Des himself had said several times recently, he had never stayed so long in one place since he was a youngster.

"I have to get going again, Ollie," he was arguing. "I'm a Traveller. I'm getting fat on all this good cooking. Not enough exercise. I can't stay here forever."

"Neither can I!" said Ollie. "OK, it was good of old Ange to take us in, and we couldn't have camped out this winter, but I'll go MAD if I have to stay in this place for much longer. Winter's just about over. Can't I come with you? Honestly, I *am* old enough! You wouldn't have to protect me, or anything stupid like that. I can fly fast and keep going. Why not?"

"Are you sure you've got over that fright in the summer, when the Humans captured you?" Des stared seriously at Ollie. "That was enough to panic any dragon."

"Course I have!" Ollie lied, crossing his tail, and not admitting that he still dreamt about his ordeal and woke in the night, sweating and terrified. It was a good thing Tom, who shared his cellar room, was such a sound sleeper! He changed his tactics. "You've got to admit I did a good job of getting rid of those Human kids. And they haven't been back, so I must have REALLY scared them."

"True. Though I seem to remember I helped!"

"PLEASE, Des! I'm sure Dad will agree if you ask him, and then we can talk Mum round. Old Ange would be glad to see the back of me. She'd like *you* to stay, though," he added, sniggering. Angelica's persistent flirting was a source of great embarrassment to Des and amusement to everyone else.

Des ignored this. "I'll think about it. I was planning to take a short trip to get my wings in trim, then to come back here to pick up Duncan and Gwen for the trip north. See them all safe to their cave. Duncan's not quite ready for such a long flight yet, but I know he's longing to get back to their glen. He may need to take it slowly with his mended wing, and he won't be up to giving Tom a lift if he needs one."

Ollie beamed. "A short trip. Just us two! Sounds perfect for a start. Where shall we go?"

"I haven't said yes! It'll be hard on Tom if you take off."

Ollie scowled. "He's OK, but he's just a kid. I can't be expected to stay and look after him. You'll be expecting me to babysit Georgie and Lily next!"

Des laughed at the thought, and clapped Ollie with one wing. "OK, I will think about it, I promise. But only if your parents agree. I'm not having you sneaking off again, even with me. Once was enough!"

A call from below brought the discussion to an end, and they headed down for food. As far as Ollie was concerned, the matter was decided. He couldn't wait to tell the others!

# Chapter 2

# A Hint of Trouble

Whenever the dragons gathered together, the kitchen felt very crowded. Angelica often took her meals up to her room when the children were particularly noisy. But today the young dragons found a serious mood prevailing. Strangely, everyone seemed to be worried about Gwen, Tom and Emily's mother. Since their arrival some weeks before, concern had centred on their father, Duncan, with his broken wing. Now that he was feeling better, it was a major problem for him to remember to be careful of it, and not risk a second break. But this time, Duncan was not the chief worry.

Gwen had eaten very little, and was sitting with drooping wings looking miserable and close to tears. When they had finished supper, the grown-ups gathered round and persuaded her to say what was troubling her. Emily, pretending she was telling her little sister a bedtime story, hid in a dark corner with Lily so that she could listen, while Alice joined Ollie and Tom down in their cellar.

"It's Nan and Edward," Gwen said in a shaky voice, sounding tearful. She was talking about her Welsh parents. "I've been wondering for a while how they've coped in this hard winter, but this morning I woke up with an awful feeling that they're in trouble. I can't get Nan out of my mind. It's as if she's calling to me. I just know there's something wrong." She stopped and sniffed, and two big tears rolled down her nose. Emily, who was very fond of her Gran, was horrified.

"What sort of place do they live in? Would they have enough shelter in the snow?" asked Alice's mother, Ellen. She had liked Nan and Edward when they had visited their family in the summer.

"It's a good place they've got," answered Des; he had known them when he was growing up in Wales. "A really deep cave halfway up a cliff on the coast.

Humans can't easily reach it, and it goes back a long way. It wouldn't get snowed up like yours in the glen. I'm sure they'll be all right, Gwen. They've lived there a long time. They know all the dangers."

"They're getting old!" Gwen refused to be comforted.

"They seemed pretty fit to me," said Oliver. "Look how far they flew in the summer."

"Pity they're not in Huff range," Duncan said. "We're nearer here than when we're at home. Could we try Huffing them, Des?"

Des shook his head. "No. There are mountains in the way." They all fell silent, wondering how best to comfort Gwen.

Old George, Alice and Ollie's grandad, had so far said nothing. He seemed to be almost in a dream, thought Emily, peering cautiously from her corner. He was a wise old dragon, and she wondered what he was thinking. When he spoke into the silence, everyone listened intently. His voice was low, and sounded somehow far away. "She calls to me too," he said.

There was a shocked silence. Emily held her breath. Unfortunately Lily, who was getting bored, chose that moment to prod her sharply with her tail, and that made her let out a shocked, "Ow!" Duncan turned and peered into the gloom.

"Emily! I thought you were downstairs with the others. Come on, Lily – bedtime." He scooped the protesting Lily from her hiding place with his good wing and Emily followed reluctantly. She looked at the still figure of Old George and then at her mum, who managed a watery smile.

"I'm probably imagining things!" she said. "I'm sure the Gramps are fine. Don't worry, Emily. Tell Tom not to be too late in bed when you go down."

Emily realised that she would learn nothing more from the circle of grown-ups. She said good-night, gave her mother an extra hug and made her way down the steep steps to the cellars, where she and the others slept. She needed to talk to them right away!

The four young dragons gathered in a huddle in the girls' room and listened in silence while Emily related all she had heard. When she had finished, Ollie and Alice looked at one another.

"Grandad's said things like that before," Alice said seriously. "He seems to sense things that nobody else can."

"And he's usually right," Ollie added. "I don't understand it. I never feel things that way. Perhaps it's some power you get when you're old."

"Mum's not that old!" Tom objected.

"I don't think it's old age. I think it's the kind of person you are," said Alice thoughtfully. "I don't get these feelings either. Do you, Emily?"

"I don't *think* so," Emily said doubtfully. She was remembering the way she and Gran could sometimes read each others' thoughts, but that was when they were together. She had never picked up a message from miles away. She decided she needed to think about this before she said anything, even to Alice.

"Anyway, the obvious thing is to fly to Wales to check on them," Ollie declared. "I bet Des is planning that right now. And he's agreed that I can travel with him when he goes off again, so I'll be going too. We can sort everything out between us, no problem. Don't worry, Em!"

The other three stared at him, open-mouthed.

"You never said!"

"I bet you haven't asked the parents!"

"That's not fair! Why can't we all go?" Tom's voice rose in outrage.

Ollie held up a wing for silence. "Shut up, you'll have them all down here! Des and I only fixed it this afternoon. Obviously we'll tell the parents, but they can't *possibly* object if I'm with Des. And it'll be better to have two of us if we're going all the way to your Gramps' place."

"Mum might want Des to take HER!" Emily interrupted, but Ollie waved this suggestion away.

"Nah, he'd prefer me to go with him, obviously," he said.

Alice scowled at him. This was the boastful brother that got on her nerves. "I don't see why," she argued. "It was ME he chose to be the leader when we were at the seaside in the summer, not you. He said you were too reckless and I was more sensible. I bet he hasn't REALLY said he'd take you. I'd prefer Gwen any day."

"Mum was great when Dad had his accident and we were waiting for Des to get back," Emily remembered. "She took charge and knew just what to do, didn't she, Tom?" Tom decided not to take sides. He was too horrified at the thought of being left behind with the girls to think about anything else.

"I'll go and find Des and we can get things organised." Ollie got up, ignoring Alice, and set off up the stairs. Alice had just time to whisper, "Honestly, he's such a...." when they all heard one word, "OUT!" shouted from upstairs. The girls collapsed in giggles, to Tom's surprise. Ollie came back down.

"They're still sitting round gassing in there. I need to talk to Des on his own," he said casually, without looking at them. "Think I'll get to bed. We might be starting early. Coming, Tom?"

"'Night!" said Alice, trying to keep the giggles at bay. "What *is* he like!" she said, turning back to Emily. Then she saw that tears were streaming down her friend's face.

"Sorry," Emily sniffed, "but it's Gran! I just know they're right and there's something the matter with her or Grandad. I want to see them again. I couldn't bear it if..." Sobs overwhelmed her again.

Alice put her wings round her. "Winter's nearly over. I'm sure they'll be OK. Des will sort things out, and he'll come back and tell us. He might even bring them back with him! You really mustn't worry!"

But looking at her friend, she realised that would not be easy.

## Chapter 3

# Ollie in a Rage

Emily slept badly that night, though she tried to keep still and quiet so she did not disturb Alice. She stopped crying, and concentrated instead on trying to pick up the 'call' from her Gran, like Gwen and George. It was not really successful, so she tried instead to send Gran a message of her own, with no real hope it would work, and then tried to think of suitable arguments to convince her parents that SHE should go to Wales with Des. Eventually she fell asleep from sheer exhaustion, and didn't even wake when Alice tiptoed out for breakfast.

Her wakening was sudden and caused by Ollie. He was rampaging round the cellar, yelling in fury, lashing his tail on the walls and sending spurts of flame to the ceiling. She staggered out, rubbing her eyes.

"Good thing the ceiling's stone down here," Alice remarked, coming over to join her. "He'd have set the place alight if there was wood, like upstairs. Watch out, idiot!" she added to Ollie as a particularly fierce flare just missed her.

"What's the matter with him?"

"Des set off to Wales last night. By himself. He said that would be quickest, so he didn't even take your Mum. He's arranged with the Dads to check out Huff range too. The grown-ups planned it all last night. That's why they wouldn't let Ollie in. He's furious, as you can hear! Turns out Des hadn't actually *promised* to take him travelling. That was just him boasting last night. Oh, GO AND HAVE YOUR TANTRUM SOMEWHERE ELSE!!" she shouted to Ollie, who was still rampaging around the cellar.

"I'm going upstairs." Emily set off for the flight of steps, trying to avoid Ollie as she went. Alice followed, and the two of them saw him disappear into the secret passage that led into the garden.

"I hope he doesn't go over the fence in a rage," Alice remarked. "That really WOULD cause a row with Dad!"

Emily had forgotten about Ollie. She was too eager to see her mother and hear about Des. She rushed into the kitchen to find her. Gwen made her sit down for a late breakfast while she told her what had been decided. "He set off soon after you went to bed," she said, bringing a bowl of porridge and adding some honey as a special treat. "He didn't take all his bundles, just some emergency rations, so he could travel light. He says he knows the quickest way."

At that moment, Oliver and Duncan came in. "You've been a long time. It's light. I hope you weren't seen!" said Ellen anxiously.

"Where've you been?" asked Emily with her mouth full.

"We've found a good Huffing spot a few miles away, up on the moor," Oliver answered. "I went a bit of the way with Des last night, and we arranged that he should send a Huff early this morning, to let us know he was OK and check we could get messages through. It worked. We picked up his Huff, and he's got a good long way. He's heading south-west, and there are lots of hills and moors that way, so he reckons he can manage to travel by day and still avoid Humans. After that, he'll reach the coast and fly out at sea to avoid being seen, until he gets to the wilds of Wales where your folks live. He's done it before. He'll come back the same way. Says it saves wasting time by hiding up during the day."

Emily beamed. "He's brilliant!" she said.

Gwen, who was looking happier this morning, chuckled. "So you always say! How does your wing feel after that flight, Duncan?"

"I managed fine, didn't I, Oliver? I reckon I could get myself home now, no bother."

"Not until we've heard from Des," his wife said firmly.

"And you need to be sure the snow has melted further north," Maggie added, bringing hot nettle tea. "Harold says there's still a lot lying, even here. It takes a long time for a big drift to disappear. We're in no hurry to be rid of you!"

"It will be quieter when we've gone!" said Duncan, hearing Tom cross the hall outside, yelling for Ollie, and Georgie and Lily scampering after him, shouting almost as loudly.

"Och, I'll miss the wee ones," said Maggie fondly.

"I'd miss Emily," Alice added. "But we'll be going back to the glen ourselves soon, won't we? We'll not be staying here as soon as it's properly spring!" She looked anxiously at her father.

"Nothing's decided yet," he said, getting up and firmly changing the subject. "Good thing we took a bag with us, Ellen. We found a heap of tatties that Humans have spilled by a track and brought some back."

"We left it outside – I'll bring it in." Duncan went out and reappeared with a bundle which he tumbled on the floor by the fire. "If these are OK we can bring some more tonight."

"I'll roast some now," said Maggie, picking them up to pierce with her talons before pushing them into the glowing embers of the fire, where they hissed and spat.

"Lovely – all black and crunchy!" said Emily, who was looking at Alice's worried face. She decided it was her turn to do some cheering-up, and finished her breakfast in a hurry.

"Shall we go out and check that Ollie hasn't done a flyer?" she whispered as they left the kitchen together.

"I suppose we'd better," Alice replied. "I can't believe he spun us that tale last night! Let's sneak round the back. He's probably just sulking."

They made their way through the front door and round to the dilapidated outhouses round the back. There was no sign of Ollie, either outside or in the ruins. Emily wondered whether he had gone back through the passage to the cellar, and ran to check, but he was nowhere to be seen. When she came back outside, Alice pointed to a heap of half-melted snow.

"He's gone into the wood!" she said. "Look, you can see the print of where he took off over the fence. I daren't shout for him in case the parents hear. I'm hoping he'll calm down out there soon and come back before he's missed."

"And before any Human sees him!" Emily added. She was worried, like Alice, but part of her wished she could go out too. Just one glimpse of their young Human friends would be wonderful!

"Where's Ollie?" Tom shouted, arriving round the corner, and was surprised when he was firmly shushed by both the girls. They explained what had happened, and Tom grinned appreciatively. "Wish he'd taken me!" he said.

"OK, we'd ALL like to go out," said Alice, rather to Emily's surprise. "But just now the important thing is to make sure nobody else discovers he's missing. We'd better all stay out here."

"We need to keep warm," Tom said. "I'll get the ball." He disappeared into the passage and the girls looked at each other and sighed. "I suppose he's got a point," said Alice. "Running around will keep us warm."

Tom re-emerged, dribbling the football that the Humans had left for him, and the three of them passed it energetically between them, with powerful tail-swipes and the occasional header. The ball was starting to feel rather soft, perhaps because their spikes were sharp.

Suddenly a particularly wild shot from Emily sent the ball flying over the fence. It disappeared into the undergrowth.

"Oh, no!" said Emily. "I suppose I'd better go over and get it, and hope nobody sees me."

"I'll go if you like," said Tom eagerly, but before Emily could argue there was a rustle in the bushes and Ollie's head appeared. He jerked it in the direction of the hidden corner and disappeared again.

The other three jumped guiltily as a voice came from above. "Where's Ollie?" Oliver, frowning suspiciously, was standing at the top of the steps looking down at them.

"Er... I swiped the ball over the fence by mistake," Emily called hurriedly. "Sorry, it was a bit wild. Ollie's just gone over to find it. He'll be back in a minute. It disappeared into the bushes, so he may have had trouble finding it..."

She was wondering how long she could keep suspicion at bay when the dark red figure of Ollie trotted casually round the corner, dribbling the ball. "Sorry, Dad – had to get this back," he said. "I was only over for a minute." Oliver stared hard at him, but then went back inside without further comment.

Ollie winked. "Quick thinking, Em!" he said. "I was just about to tell one of you to send it over and give me an excuse to be out when the ball flew over and hit me! Thanks." He seemed to have left his bad temper behind in the woods, Emily thought. It was rare that Ollie ever praised one of them, so she felt rather pleased with herself.

"Nice to see you've quietened down a bit," said Alice coldly. "Maybe you'll think twice before swaggering again. And running away!" she added with her nose in the air.

"Perhaps," said Ollie, with a maddening smirk, "but if I hadn't '*run away*', I'd have missed a Human sighting. Course, if you're not interested..."

Emily gave Alice a prod with her tail. "'Course we are!" she said, and led the way through the passage and into their cellar, leaving the rest to follow. Alice, still disapproving, came last.

# Chapter 4

# Quarrels

The four young dragons settled themselves in the girls' cellar, and Emily produced a secret stash of bumblebugs. She hoped it would help to soothe the prickles between Alice and Ollie. "How far did you go?" she asked.

"Not that far. I went to Ben's Stone to start with," Ollie said, referring to the huge boulder in the wood that Ben McIlwhinnie had rested on before starting the journey back to his glen. "Ben's footprints have melted away, but you can see something big has been through the trees if you know where to look. Turned out it wasn't much use as a look-out point, because of the trees, so I flew further on, low between the tree trunks keeping a good look-out. Nothing moving anywhere, apart from the odd wee bird, and not much snow left. I thought I'd head in the direction of that Human house, just to see how far it was."

Alice rolled her eyes in exasperation. "Why do you take such risks? You could just as well have gone the other way!"

"Shut up, Allie!" said Emily, unexpectedly. "Go on, Ollie. Did you find it?"

"It took quite a while to get to the edge of the wood," Ollie continued. "When the trees thinned I dropped to the ground and crawled through the undergrowth. And THEN...." he dropped his voice conspiratorially and they all leaned closer, "I came to one of those hard tracks..."

"A road?" said Emily.

"Yeah, just a narrow one. Then I had a REAL fright!" He paused for dramatic effect.

"What happened?"

"One of those Human machines thundered past, right in front of me! It was a big one, bright colours, and I could see some Humans inside, looking out."

"Wow!" said Tom, lost in admiration.

"You weren't seen, were you?" Alice cried in horror.

"Nah – it went by too fast. But THEN...."

"Yes...?"

"It stopped a bit further down the road-thing. And I saw two young Humans run out into the road and climb on. And guess who it was!"

"Not Lisa?" Emily cried.

"Ssshh!" said Alice, looking over her shoulder at the open doorway.

"Lisa and that little one," said Ollie triumphantly.

"Charlie? The one who told me about football?" said Tom.

"Both of them. They were carrying bags and when they had disappeared into the machine it went away round the corner, and I couldn't see it any more. Pretty good spying though, eh?" He sat back, beaming in triumph, and allowed Tom to give him a High Four. Emily and Alice looked at one another.

"I think the big machine might have been a... a 'bus'," said Alice thoughtfully. "Remember that story, Emily? In the book they gave us?"

"Of course it was!" said Emily excitedly. "And I bet they were going to School, like we've read about.

Where they learn things and have fun all together. They were carrying their School Bags! That must have been a School Bus. Wow, Ollie, you've seen an actual School Bus! You are SO lucky! I wish I'd seen it…"

"Come out with me tomorrow if you like. It might come along again," said Ollie, trying to sound casual, but obviously delighted with all the excitement he had caused.

It was obvious that Emily was seriously tempted. Alice looked horrified.

"Don't be stupid! We can't! You think you were lucky this time, Ollie, but you don't KNOW some of the Humans on the bus didn't spot something bright red in the undergrowth. What if they mention it and that wee Charlie lets something out about us? He might say 'must have been a dragon!' and Lisa would try to cover up and who knows WHAT the others would think. We might have search parties out in the woods. There's no way we should risk it again."

It was obvious that she was deadly serious. And angry. Tom looked from her to Emily, wondering how to break the tension building up in the small room. "I'm hungry," he said. "Let's go and find a snack."

"Me too!" said Alice, and turned from the others to head upstairs. "Come on, Tom," she added over her shoulder. Emily felt rather hurt and a bit upset by her attitude. After all, she had not taken Ollie up on his offer! But as she turned to follow them, Ollie touched her arm. "Find out all you can about School Buses from those books of yours," he whispered. "Then we'll sneak out and see it again. We'll be careful. Don't tell the others. Come on! You know you want to!"

He gave her a wicked grin before he headed upstairs, leaving Emily in a very muddled state of mind.

Things were rather tense between the four of them for the rest of the day. Ollie's deliberately casual swagger was irritating Alice unbearably, and she was snappy with everyone and avoided Emily. Tom, obviously rather bemused by the atmosphere, practised Tail-Stane shots endlessly, annoying everyone, especially Aunt Angelica, who was never happy when the peace of her 'castle' was so rudely disturbed. Lily, sensing tension, decided to have a couple of her famous tantrums. Gwen was obviously still very worried, and Duncan was, equally obviously, itching to be back home in the glen. They all missed the cheerful presence of Des; nobody knew how long it would be before he returned, and there could be no news now that he was well outside the range of Huff signals.

For once, Emily was glad when it was bed-time. She hoped that Alice had got over her bad mood and would become her cheerful and sensible friend again. At first this seemed likely as they settled down as usual on their beds. But then Alice spotted the book that Emily pulled from under the hay.

"That's the book about the children at school that Lisa and Megan gave us!" she hissed. "You're reading up about School Buses, aren't you? You're planning to go out with Ollie! I can't believe it! I know HE'S stupid, but I never thought YOU'D risk our freedom like that. I've a good mind to tell Mum and Dad!"

"I HAVEN'T said I'd go out with Ollie!" Emily protested.

"But you'd like to!"

"Yes I would!" Emily began to lose her temper. She felt that Alice was being unfair. "And if I do, and you tell, I'll never speak to you again!" She turned her back on Alice and pretended to read her book, but she was so angry and upset that the words blurred on the page. She hoped that Alice would say sorry and promise never to tell, but after a few minutes of tense silence, she heard Alice flounce over in bed, turning her back as well. She found the pages that mentioned the School Bus and read all she could find. She would sneak a word with Ollie in the morning!

She read on defiantly, too irritated to sleep, until she realised that Alice was snoring faintly on the other side of the room. When she finally put the book away, having found out as much as she could, she still couldn't sleep. She made up her mind, slid off her bed and tiptoed quietly across the cellar to the room where the boys slept. She would wake Ollie and make a plan with him now, while nobody could hear her!

At the arched doorway of the boys' cellar room, she hesitated. In the faint moonlight shining through a tiny high window, she could see the humped shape of Tom, motionless in his bed, but Ollie was thrashing about in a muddle of hay and straw, swishing his tail and muttering. She heard a few blurred words – "Can't move!" "No, NO...!" and realised that Ollie was in the grip of a nightmare. She knew what *that* felt like! She was just about to move in and wake him when he gave a final heave and a low cry and she saw that he had woken himself up. She held her breath, expecting Tom to wake too, but he just stirred and slept on. At the same time, Ollie, shaking his head and breathing heavily, realised she was there.

"Em!" he said, confused. "What you doing here? I...I...thought I..."

"It's all right," Emily whispered, moving into the room. "You were dreaming, I think. Are you OK?" She could sense him shivering.

"Course I am! Didn't wake you, did I? Allie's not out there too?"

"No. I wasn't asleep. I've been reading the School Bus book. I came to say I'd like to go out to see it, if you'll come too. Alice doesn't approve, so could we sneak out without telling her?"

"Course we could! Great!" Ollie was recovering fast. "What have you found out?"

Emily sat next to him on the hay. "It happens twice every day. The bus picks up all the children from their caves – houses I mean - in the morning and takes them to the school-place. Then they go home in the afternoon. Except for two days they call the 'week-end'. I don't know what that means."

"Not at night?"

"No."

"Pity. Makes it more difficult for two of us to sneak out. We need to think about this. Can't decide tonight, but good idea of yours to come and tell me. I'll work something out. Better get back in case Allie wakes and notices you're missing. Tom never does, fortunately!"

"I hope you don't have another nightmare," said Emily as she got up. "They can be horrible! Are you sure you're OK?"

"I'm fine, honestly. Don't say anything, will you? You know how they fuss!"

"I won't. 'Night." She tiptoed across to her own room and fell asleep as soon as she hit the hay. Ollie lay down, took several deep calming breaths, stared into the darkness and tried very hard to stay awake.

# Chapter 5

# The Rook–Hunt

Emily slept so late the following morning that her mother came down to the cellar to check on her. She was just surfacing, and remembering the events of the previous day – and the night – when she saw Gwen in the doorway.

"Are you feeling all right? The others came up a while ago. What's the matter with Alice? She's hardly said a word. You haven't been quarrelling, have you?"

Emily shook herself free of her hay. Her bed was in a mess, so she had obviously been tossing and turning. "Not really," she said, wondering what to say. She obviously couldn't tell her mother the real reason. Gwen looked sympathetic, which made her feel guilty.

"It wouldn't be surprising," she said. "You've been cooped up together for a long time now. I'm surprised you haven't started fighting. And I'm really amazed that Angelica hasn't turned us out before now. Especially on indoor Tail-Stane days!"

"If only we could go out for a proper fly!" said Emily as they crossed to the stairs. "I'd love to explore round here before we go back to the Glen. When do you think Des will be back?"

"Not yet. It would take him at least two days to get there, even at his speed. And we don't know if he'll need to stay. It's hard to wait for news, isn't it?" Looking at her mother, Emily realised it was even harder for her, and gave her a quick hug.

"I'll try not to fight with Alice! Sorry!" she said.

"What for?" Fortunately they had reached the kitchen and Gwen didn't seem to be expecting an answer. Oliver was just coming in through the hole in the front door.

"It's getting warmer outside. Thick mist out there, so we might manage to get them out. What do you think?" he addressed Gwen, but Emily listened open-mouthed.

"Us?" she asked, breathlessly.

"Breakfast!" said her mother firmly, pushing her through the door. Oliver bounded up the stairs to the tower room in search of Duncan.

It was hard to see inside the kitchen, which was full of smoke from the fire mixing with mist drifting in through the window. Alice was playing a game with Lily and Georgie and didn't look up, but Ollie gave her a searching glance from the other side of the room.

"You're late!" said Tom. Emily ignored him and sat down with a bowl of porridge.

Alice stalked across the room followed by the little dragons, falling over each other and both talking at once. "Tom, we're going to set up that run with the wee balls in the other room," she called. "Not enough room in here. Coming?"

Tom, who had found a bag of marbles while rummaging in the upstairs cupboard in a fruitless search for another tennis ball, agreed and followed them across the hall. Gwen looked at Ellen and raised significant eyes to the ceiling. Ellen shook her head and shrugged her wings. Emily was scowling as she finished her porridge. Ollie finished stacking a pile of firewood and looked thoughtfully at her.

"Shall I take Grandad a drink?" he offered. His mother looked surprised. "Thanks, Ollie. Here you are. He's probably better staying in his room as it's so foggy and damp."

"Can I go and say hallo to him?" Emily asked. She was very fond of Old George. As Ellen nodded, she vanished into the hall after Ollie. Their mothers stared suspiciously after them.

"There's certainly something going on!" said Ellen. "I agree – they need to get out! Let's hope Duncan and Oliver decide it would be safe."

Emily headed for the stairs, following Ollie. Once he had delivered the tea, they might have a chance to talk over their plan. Old George looked drowsy, but twinkled his thanks to them both as they left him to rest in his little room. It was the only room with a window intact, so was always cosy and warm. They paused for a whispered consultation before going down the stairs, but were almost knocked over by the flurry of Duncan and Oliver hurtling down from the tower.

"What's up?" asked Ollie.

"Great flock of rooks just gone over," Oliver said over his shoulder as he followed Duncan down the stairs. "They've settled in the trees outside. Worth a hunt."

Ollie and Emily looked at each other, then dashed down the stairs after them and followed them through the hole in the door. The mist outside was so thick they could hardly make out the fence at the edge of the garden.

"We can't possibly be seen in this, Dad," Ollie panted. "We could help..."

"No harm, I suppose," said Oliver to Duncan, who nodded.

"All right," he said. "Listen. This is what we do..." Quietly he explained that they had to fly all together above the trees, space out and drop all at once into the mass of birds in the treetops, taking them by surprise. "Swipe as many as you can with your tails as they take off in fright," he added. "Dead or stunned, they'll tumble to the ground and we can collect them up when the flock's gone. Should manage a fair few before they escape. OK? Ready?"

"You've done this once before, remember Ollie?" said Oliver. "You haven't, have you Emily? Sure you want to have a try?"

"Course I do!" said Emily. Duncan looked pleased. "Just don't get your tail tangled in the branches," he said.

"We'll come and rescue you if you do!" added Ollie, and Emily gave him a friendly punch as Oliver gave the signal to take off. She had quite forgotten about Alice!

They took off as quietly as possible, with Duncan bringing up the rear, and headed into the mist away from the trees. They soon lost sight of the ground, and then even the tops of the trees disappeared into the blanketing mist. Oliver wheeled round and headed for the wood. Emily could see nothing, but gradually the raucous chattering of the rooks could be heard below them. When Duncan had reached the spot, he signalled to Emily and the others to space out. They all hovered silently, then dived together.

Taken by surprise, and calling in alarm, the rooks rose in a mass, and the four dragons dived into the flock, tails swinging. Emily had no idea how many birds she hit, but she closed her eyes tightly and felt her tail connect with battering wings. It felt as though she was lost inside a whirling black cloud, but it actually only took a couple of minutes before the flock had departed, still shrieking furiously, and she realised she was in danger of tangling herself in the higher branches. Just before that happened, her father loomed out of the mist and beckoned her to follow him. The dragons regrouped in the air, and Oliver led them safely through the trees to the ground below.

Ollie and Emily were breathless but beaming and excited, especially when they found the place where the rooks had fallen and realised how many were lying on the ground beneath the trees. "Well done, you two!" said Duncan. "Looks like a good number."

"You collect the ones here, and I'll check for any lodged in the branches," said Oliver. "No point risking your wing, Duncan." A few minutes later they gathered together and inspected their haul. They each took two or three rooks in each claw and prepared to fly back.

"D'you think they'll come back?" asked Ollie, obviously longing to repeat the experience.

"Not for a while," said his father. "But we might make the most of this mist while it lasts." The fence loomed in front of them, and they flew over and landed at the top of the steps. "Leave them in a pile," Duncan said. "In you go!"

Emily and Ollie gave a triumphant High Four before scrambling back into the house. Emily felt fantastic. She couldn't wait to tell Alice. Then she remembered their quarrel and her excitement died. She should have waited and told Alice, so that she could go rook-hunting too. Now she felt guilty. Perhaps she should keep quiet. But it was too late. Ollie crashed into the kitchen.

"Guess what we've been doing!" he yelled triumphantly.

## Chapter 6

# Alice in a Huff

The grown-ups in the kitchen seemed to be delighted with the pile of rooks, even though it meant a lot of plucking and a great mess of feathers. They were working fast through their food stocks. Predictably, Angelica failed to appear, but Oliver came down from George's room to say that his father would be happy to pluck rooks in his room, and he would keep the feathers to make his bed softer. He headed upstairs with a large armful.

Emily decided she could put it off no longer, and went to look for Alice. Tom had already rushed into the kitchen to hear the news. Lily and Georgie were tail-swiping marbles and scampering after them at the other end of the room, but Alice was sitting on

her aunt's splendid couch with her arms and wings folded, and a scowl on her face. Emily sighed. "I'm sorry we went without you," she said. "It all happened so fast. The Dads said we had to hurry before the rooks flew away. There was no time to come and look for you...." Her voice trailed away.

"You left me out on purpose!" said Alice, coldly. "You went off with *Ollie*..." her voice was full of scorn, but before Emily could think of an answer that wouldn't make the quarrel worse, Ellen appeared in the doorway.

"I don't want to know what this is all about," she said, "but Oliver and Duncan have an idea. They want you in the kitchen; BOTH of you – now!" She vanished again, and a relieved Emily rushed after her. Alice hesitated, then followed more slowly. Annoyed though she was, she did not want to be left out again!

She found everyone gathered in the kitchen listening to Oliver. "....need to make the most of this mist. It's not lifting at all – getting thicker, if anything. We don't reckon it would be too risky for a lot of us to go out foraging. There's the field where the pigeons gather for a start. Maybe pheasants - Duncan and I saw quite a few wandering about yesterday morning. They're never around at night, when Des and I go out. Pheasant would make a nice change!"

"There's the tattie field too. And snails might be coming out," Duncan added. "We'll be lucky to find any berries, but no harm keeping an eye out."

"Do you want to take the children?" Gwen asked.

"I think you should ALL go," said Maggie. "Do you good. You're not used to being cooped up inside. I can see to these rooks if George gives me a hand, and the wee ones seem happy enough. I'll feed them when they get hungry, and you can take some food with you. Harold's out the back breaking firewood. He said he'd leave some sticks for Tom to jump in the cellar."

"The important thing is that nobody goes off alone," said Ellen. "We need to stay in small groups, and make sure we keep listening out for danger. We'll hear Humans before we see them today, and that will give us a chance to hide or get clear."

"And at the first sign of the mist lifting, we head straight back here," Duncan added. "No hanging around."

"I take it you kids want to come?" Oliver said, grinning round at the expectant faces.

"Yes PLEASE!" said Emily. Tom punched the air in wild relief at not being left behind with the wee ones, and Alice managed to look a bit more cheerful.

"We'll stick to the rules," Ollie promised unexpectedly, then, when everyone looked at him, astonished, he added, "Someone's got to take Des's place while he's away."

"Good. Let's get going. Over the fence and through the woods to Ben's Stone. We'll gather there and decide how to split up." Oliver led the way through the front door.

"Could my lad be learning a bit of sense at last?" Ellen murmured to Gwen as they watched their children pass through the hole one by one.

"Hmm – trying to take Des's place? I don't recall *him* sticking to any rules!" Gwen replied, and they both chuckled as they followed the others outside.

She took a deep breath. "It's nice to be going outside again, even in mist as thick as this!" she said as they took off together, bringing up the rear.

They settled in a group on the huge stone and waited for Oliver, who had flown out to check on the field where the pigeons gathered. When he came back they made plans. "There are enough there to make it worth a raid," he said. "I'll take Ollie. On my way I could hear quite a lot of rustling in the undergrowth, so I think there may be pheasants there. If you three kids could spread out and try to drive them into the open, Gwen and Ellen can catch and dispatch. OK?" They all nodded.

"I think it's worth a trip to that big pond. I'll check there are no Humans around, then see if there are any fish," Duncan added thoughtfully. "Tom, you're the best in the water. Why don't you come with me? Two should be enough to drive pheasants out of cover." Tom beamed with pride and stretched out his wings.

"Stick close to your Dad," Gwen warned, looking slightly worried as Tom took off with Duncan. They were soon out of sight among the trees. Ollie and his father left next, heading in the opposite direction, and flying higher to avoid disturbing any pheasants too soon.

"Right you two," said Ellen, choosing to ignore the chill that remained between the girls. "We've done this before – remember, Alice? Fly low and slowly, and swish your tail in the undergrowth. You could try the odd huff – the ground's so wet there's no risk of starting a fire. The birds usually scuttle out into the open before they fly, and that's when we can get them. Give us a few minutes to get to the edge of the wood and check the place is clear of Humans. Huff's no use in this mist, so I'll call. Keep a lookout for anything else worth foraging on the way. All right?"

The girls nodded and watched them fly into the trees. They didn't speak, but stared ahead, listening for a signal, tense and waiting. When they heard a low cry they set off, spaced out but keeping each other in sight. Emily watched as Alice flew ahead, and copied her flight action. She could hear rustling noises below her as she swung her tail, and then a sudden loud honk that she knew was a startled cock pheasant. It felt as though they would never reach the edge of the wood. But soon she heard unmistakeable alarm calls from the trees ahead, and as she and Alice burst into the open, she saw the dim figures of Gwen and Ellen through the mist.

There was a tangled confusion of tails, beaks, wings and feathers in the grassy clearing. Several more pheasants burst from the shelter of the trees and launched themselves clumsily into the air, flying low. As Emily came to land, a red-brown streak raced into the open and snatched the last pheasant out of the air with an amazing leap. A fox! It came to earth with its mouth full of pheasant, dropped to all fours and came trotting back. "Nice bit o' beatin'!" it said thickly through the feathers and disappeared into the undergrowth.

"Cheek!" said Gwen. "I was just about to grab that one!"

"That's foxes for you!" said Ellen. "I've had them raid our camp before, and they often swipe rabbits we've found. Never mind, we got two each – that's not bad." As she spoke, two smaller birds crept from the undergrowth. The girls expected them to be pounced on, but Ellen simply waved them away with a wing, and the two took off together, their wings whirring, and disappeared into the mist. "Partridges," she said. "I never like killing a partridge. You always see two together, or a family group. Pheasants are different. They're bred specially for Humans to kill, so why shouldn't we have them instead?"

"Perhaps we'd better get these home, in case that fox fancies another," said Gwen. "They're heavy – can you girls manage to carry one each?" They nodded but had no breath for speaking as they flew back to the castle, and each squeezed a feathered bundle through the door and into the hall.

Maggie was delighted. "Goodness, what a feast we'll have!" she said. "They should keep a few days if we hang them in the cellar. We don't need them tonight." Emily suspected that she wanted to be sure Des would not miss barbecued pheasant.

"Have the others been back?" Gwen asked, as they all had a welcome drink, but Maggie shook her head.

"Want to go out again?" Ellen asked.

The girls agreed. "More pheasants?" asked Emily.

"Course not!" said Alice with a trace of scorn. "They may be pretty brainless, but they won't be back in that bit of wood for a while."

"What else shall we try then?"

"We'll take the bags and see what we can find," Ellen decided. "I think I spotted some big fungus discs on old birch trees while we were flying through. That's always worth collecting, if we can find it again. Come on!"

There was still no sign of the others as they flew back over the fence.

## Chapter 7

# Snails and a School Bus

To Emily's surprise, Ellen led them straight to the birch trees with the fungus growing out of the trunk like shelves. She obviously had a very good memory, and was an expert forager. Some of the fungus was rotten, but there was enough that she declared edible for them to fill one of the bags quite quickly. Gwen flew back home to empty it, while Ellen led the girls to a glade with several fallen tree-trunks lying half buried in the weeds and brambles.

"You can find lots of goodies in a rotting tree-trunk," she said. "Bugs, slugs, beetles – all sorts."

"I know," said Alice. "You've shown me before." Her mother, recognising a sulk when she heard one, ignored her, and addressed Emily instead.

"Dig your claws into the cracks and prise them apart. You'll usually find something worth eating inside. Scrabble underneath – that's where the snails hibernate. You two tackle this log while I go on a bit and find another."

"I'll go and find my own log," Alice said, and disappeared before anyone could argue. Ellen looked at Emily's crestfallen expression, and patted her wing. "She'll get over it!" she said. "You have a good look here. Your Mum will be back in a minute." She disappeared after Alice, and Emily sighed heavily before starting to hunt. Alice's bad mood was ruining their day out! She wondered how Tom and Ollie were getting on, and wished she had been allowed to go with one of them instead.

By the time Gwen came back with her empty bag, she was feeling more cheerful. She had discovered a sizeable colony of hibernating snails clustered under the log. Between them, they prised a number out and put them in the bag. "Don't take them all," Gwen reminded her. Further along the log Emily tripped over a rolled-up hedgehog hidden under a drift of leaves, and accidentally kicked it into open ground, spiking her foot in the process. Her startled yelp brought Ellen back from her own foraging, and she helped Gwen roll the sleeping animal back into its nest. "Soon be waking and needing those snails. Good thing you left a few," she remarked, patting the leaves over it and departing.

"I wonder how Dad and Tom are getting on," Emily said as they resumed their scavenging.

"Oh, they got back just as I was coming out again," said Gwen. "Both soaking wet, of course, but they'd caught quite a few wee fish. Nothing like the trout in our loch, but I expect they'll be quite tasty. They decided to stay and warm up. Duncan wouldn't admit it, but I think his wing was aching. And there was no way Maggie was letting Tom out again until he'd stopped shivering!" Emily chuckled, imagining Tom enjoying the fuss, boasting about his fishing and wheedling snacks out of Maggie.

They carried on digging into the rotten wood and underneath the logs, and found a variety of edible bugs and beetles for a pot of Gwen's favourite broth.

Emily was starting to get bored collecting snails, and was wondering whether she was ready to go back, when there was a crashing in the branches above her head and Ollie dropped to the ground beside her. "We've got loads of pigeons," he said happily, stealing a couple of large snails from Emily's collection and crunching loudly. "Then Dad took me right to the signalling moor, in case there was a Huff from Des. There wasn't, but we bagged a couple of rabbits on the way back. And we got some more tatties from the pile. Good, eh?" He perched on the log while Emily finished filling her bag.

Oliver appeared and admired Gwen and Emily's collection. "Alice has found quite a lot of berries deep inside a hawthorn bush. A bit dried and wrinkled, but they'll flavour a stew. She collected some rose-hips too. She's just headed home to hide them before Ollie sees them. Are you ready to go? I think Ellen is. We've done really well!"

"Yes, I think we can call it a day," said Gwen. "It's been good to be out, but I'm getting chilly."

"Dad!" Ollie interrupted, scrambling off the log. "Shall I just fly round the track on the way home to see if there are any of those knobbly root-things the Humans have dropped? Harold said they were as good as tatties. Might as well, while we're out. I know the way home, and it's not far."

"I suppose so. The mist's not lifted so you should be OK. We've seen nothing of Humans all day. Don't take any risks, though!"

"I'll be careful. Want to come with me, Em?"

"Can I, Mum?"

"All right, but don't be too long." Emily beamed. "Don't tell Alice!" she whispered in her Mum's ear, and took off with Ollie before anyone could change their minds.

"Perfect!" said Ollie as soon as they were out of earshot. "Just the chance we needed. The track's near that road-thing, and if we're quick we could sneak a look at the house our Human kids live in as well. Come on!" The grown-up and responsible forager had disappeared, and the reckless Ollie was back. Emily put all thoughts of Alice out of her mind and crossed her talons as she flew. She just MIGHT catch a glimpse of Lisa!

It did not take them long to reach the muddy track which wound round the edge of the wood. Ollie turned and headed down it, pausing once to swoop and snatch up a large muddy lump of a vegetable that lay abandoned beside the track. "This'll keep Dad happy," he said, flying back to Emily. "Careful now, the road's just a bit further on. When we get to those trees ahead, we land and creep."

The sun had not broken through the mist all day and now Emily was aware that it was beginning to get a bit darker. As they landed, Ollie left his vegetable by the track and crept cautiously through the undergrowth. Emily followed. They stopped at the edge of the hard road and looked in both directions. Ollie pointed, and Emily saw with excitement that the roof of a Human house could be seen above the hedge a few yards from where they crouched. She was just about to whisper, "Is that Lisa's?" when the ground seemed to shake and they heard a distant rumble.

Emily held her breath. The two dragons flattened themselves into the weeds and grasses and peered in the direction of the noise. Then, round the corner, came the School Bus! It stopped, with a sigh that made it sound almost alive, Emily thought, and she almost leapt into the air with excitement as two children climbed down into the road. Ollie took a grip of her arm, as though he realised she might jump and risk being seen.

Lisa and Charlie were in full view. Both of them swung bags on their shoulders, and waved to the Bus as it moved off. The dragons crouched even lower as the Bus picked up speed, roared inches past their hiding place, and disappeared down the road in a cloud of smelly fumes. When Emily's ears stopped ringing, she opened her eyes again; but when she risked a glance at the house, Lisa and Charlie had gone.

Ollie was beaming triumphantly at her. "How about that? Bet you've never seen a Bus as close as that before."

They both stared along the road in the direction of the vanished Bus, and Emily thought she could still hear a distant rumble. She sighed. "I wish Lisa had stayed in the road a bit longer!"

"You're never satisfied!" Ollie complained, and she grinned ruefully and agreed.

At that moment, a voice spoke from the undergrowth behind them. "Howway, if it isna' the birdie-bashers!" Startled, they whirled round, ready to fly and came face to face with the fox. It was sitting in the grass, licking its lips and looking smug. Although it was red, there was grey round its muzzle, so it was quite an elderly beast, Emily realised.

"You didn't eat that *whole pheasant*!" said Emily, outraged. "He grabbed one of ours!" she told Ollie.

The fox grinned. "Nah, took it home to share wi' the missus. Ah ate a good chunk though. Nice easy catch! Ah'm off te see what's in the bin at the Human place over yonder. Fancy comin' along?"

"Is it safe?"

"Course it is! Thiz a coupla dogs, but Ah'm faster – if they try te chase me Ah'm off through the fence like a shot. The wee ones there like te see me, so Ah stick around times, give a caper or two to keep 'em happy. Humans, eh? Nae brains!"

It was obvious that Emily was seriously tempted, and for once it was Ollie who kept his head. "Can't," he said. "Got to stay hidden from Humans. Matter of life and death. We'd risk a zoo if we were spotted."

"Pity," said the fox. "Ah'd like to see their faces if they spotted you two dancin' on their grass! Ye're livin' in that old ruin in the wood, aren't ye? Used to prowl round there before ye came, then Ah saw one o' ye breathing flames and decided no' te bother. Aye well, see y' around." He trotted past them and sauntered casually down the middle of the road. "Thanks for the birdie!" he added over his shoulder as he leapt the gate into the garden of the children's house.

"It must make life easy if Humans know you exist," Emily said sadly as she and Ollie took off and headed for home, collecting their turnip on the way. "No need to hide or keep watch all the time. It was the same for the otters. They didn't mind if they were spotted."

"I don't think it's that easy, even for them," Ollie said. "There were otters in that Safari Park place, remember? Humans just like keeping things in cages.

The grown-up ones are *horrible*." He sounded bitter and angry, and Emily looked at him thoughtfully, suddenly remembering his nightmare of the previous night.

"Thank you for showing me the School Bus," she said awkwardly. "It was really exciting, just like in a book. And it was great seeing Lisa and Charlie, even for a minute."

Ollie shed his bitter mood. "Yeah – and they had no idea we were there! I told you we could do it. " He grinned triumphantly. "Just don't let on to the Parents!"

## Chapter 8

# News from Wales

E mily and the others slept much more soundly that night, tired after their energetic day
and full of Maggie's rook and tattie stew. In
the morning, Alice seemed to have recovered a little
of her usual cheerfulness, and the late return of Ollie and Emily was not mentioned. It was still misty,
though not as thick as the day before. The children
hoped for another day's foraging outside the fence,
but the grown-ups decided that the stores were full
enough.

"What about firewood?" Ollie suggested hopefully,
and as Harold agreed that he could do with some help,
the three older ones were allowed to go a little way
into the wood and fly to and fro over the fence with
branches. Tom set to work jumping the sticks into

useable sizes in the cellar; it had always been his favourite job in their glen. Nobody mentioned Humans.

As the day wore on, Emily began to hope that Des was on his way home. She was longing for news of her Gramps, but bedtime came and there was still no sign of him. She tried not to fall asleep, without success, but managed to wake early and crept upstairs before the others were awake. Duncan and Oliver were just coming in from the garden.

"Is Des back?" she asked, breathlessly.

"The mist's cleared and we picked up a Huff. He's on his way," Duncan assured her.

"He'll be a few hours yet, "Oliver added.

"Did he say the Gramps are OK?"

"Too far away to be clear. He'll tell us when he gets here. You just have to be patient!" Her father put a wing round her as they went into the kitchen to give the news to Gwen.

After breakfast, Emily decided to go up to the tower room to watch for Des. She couldn't settle to anything else. The others were having a late breakfast as she slipped away on her own. She perched on the edge of the Western window and gazed out, willing a grubby green dragon to appear. The trees hid most of the view, but peering sideways, she could just see the roof and chimneys of Lisa's house in the distance. There was a thin trickle of smoke coming from one of them, and she fell into a dream, wondering if Lisa was sitting by the fire reading a book. Perhaps it was a mysterious 'weekend' and she was at home. Or was she on that noisy bus on her way to School...?

She jumped as Alice appeared in the doorway and almost tumbled out of the window. Hurriedly she scanned for Des, but there was still no sign of him.

"Dad says he thinks he'll be a while yet," Alice said, perching on the South window and gazing out too. "Maggie's planning a welcome feast. She's got Tom and Ollie preparing all those fish, threading them on sticks ready for the fire. And Mum's making the rest of the rooks into rissoles."

"Yummy!" said Emily. Ellen's crunchy rook rissoles were a favourite of hers. She stared out of the window again and sighed. Still no Des!

Alice broke the silence awkwardly. "I wouldn't REALLY have told Mum and Dad, you know," she said, gazing out of her window without looking at Emily. "Sorry I've been in such a bad mood."

Emily felt a rush of relief, and turned to look at Alice. "I'm sorry too," she said. "I didn't mean to leave you out of the rook-hunt, honestly."

Alice turned and smiled. "Let's blame Ollie!" she said. "You are SO lucky that Tom's younger than you. Big brothers are a real pain! He drives me mad when he boasts all the time and swaggers around pretending he's so special."

"Little brothers can be a pain too," Emily said. "Let's forget the boys and look for Des. I can't wait to see him and hear about my Gramps!" Alice nodded, satisfied. It was not the time to tell her about the second sighting of the School Bus, Emily thought, turning back to her look-out and feeling only a tiny twinge of guilt. Gwen, coming up half an hour later to check for Des herself, felt the friendlier atmosphere between them, and decided to leave them to their watch. "Peace restored for now!" she reported to Ellen as she re-entered the kitchen, and they both breathed a sigh of relief.

Alice and Emily almost missed the arrival of Des. Gazing at the sky, they forgot that he was likely to weave his way through the trees to stay hidden, and he was almost at the fence when they spotted him. They made a dash for the stairs, and arrived in the hall just as he squeezed through the door and flopped in an exhausted heap on the floor. He hardly seemed to notice as Ollie appeared from the kitchen and between them they hauled him through into the warmth by the fire. They had never seen him looking so grey and limp.

"Is he all right?" Emily whispered to her mother, worried by his closed eyes and laboured breathing.

"I think he's just exhausted," Gwen whispered back. "Stay back and keep quiet." The children retreated, subdued and anxious. They had expected a triumphant return. This wasn't the Des they knew! They watched in silence as Gwen picked up a mug of steaming nettle tea, and sat down beside Des. "Drink this!" she said quietly, and to their relief Des stirred, put out a claw, drained the tea and slowly opened his eyes. He looked up into Gwen's anxious face.

"You were right," he said softly, speaking only to Gwen, so the others had to strain their ears. "Nan is ill. When I arrived I found her very weak. Edward is looking after her as best he can. Their food stocks were low, but I went hunting for them, and by the time I left Nan was a bit stronger. Edward hopes she will get better as the weather warms up. They have enough food now. They wanted me to come back to tell you." He stopped, looking exhausted, and stared at Gwen, whose face was running with tears. "I'm sorry!" he said, and closed his eyes.

Ellen came forward. "Food or sleep, Des?" she said briskly. "We can hear more later."

"Sleep," said Des, taking another mug of tea. "Food after, OK?" He heaved himself to his feet with an effort. "I'll be fine!" he said, looking at the ring of anxious faces and trying to raise a smile. "Just make sure you keep Ange away..." He staggered towards the stairs, and Oliver followed to make sure he reached his tower safely. Maggie had sent Harold ahead with an armful of fresh hay for his bed.

A silence fell in the kitchen. Emily ran to her mother, who was still sitting on the floor by the fire. Without being asked, Alice collected the little dragons and motioned to Tom and Ollie to join her. "Nothing too noisy!" warned Ellen as they left the kitchen, and Alice nodded.

Duncan joined Gwen and a tearful Emily. "I want to go and see Gran!" she wailed.

"I know. And so do I," her mother said. "But it isn't easy. You saw the state of Des, and he's a Traveller!"

"We could take it more slowly."

"We can't decide anything until we hear more detail from Des," said Duncan. Ellen, bringing tea for everyone, nodded her agreement, and they all turned as Oliver returned. Old George was with him.

"So the Call was a true one," he said to Gwen, sitting beside her close to the fire. "She will send again if she needs you, you can be sure of that. No need of Huff if you can hear the Call." Emily gazed at his wise kindly face and wondered if she would ever be able to hear the Call. Now that she knew about it, she would practise listening, she thought.

"This complicates things," said Duncan to Ellen and Oliver. "I had pretty well decided it was time to take the family back to the Glen. We can take it in easy stages, so my wing should be OK."

"But that will take us further from Wales!" Gwen said despondently, and Duncan nodded.

Emily looked at each of the grown-ups in turn, hoping to hear that the others would be coming too, but nobody said anything. Old George guessed what she was thinking. "It's too early to think of camping," he said. "There may still be snow in your glen. We should wait to hear from Des when he wakes. He flew over mountains on his way to Wales, so he will have a better idea of whether it is safe for you to return."

Just then the quietly sympathetic atmosphere in the kitchen was rudely shattered. The door was flung wide dramatically and Angelica made her usual grand entrance, breathing ominous flames.

"I hear from Maggie that Desmond has returned. None of you had the courtesy to tell me!"

"He brought bad news," Ellen said, in an obvious attempt to calm her down. "Gwen's mother is ill, in Wales."

"Well I hope you don't intend to bring her here!" said Angelica haughtily. "I think I have taken in enough *cave-dwelling* dragons this winter. It is enough that my father needs to be looked after."

"I haven't noticed YOU doing any of the 'looking after'! You leave it to Maggie," said Oliver, before anyone else could speak. George shook his head at him and waved a wing for quiet.

"No discussion until Desmond is awake. And it certainly is no time for quarrelling. Nobody should leave until the time is right."

Angelica snorted and flounced out, leaving behind a waft of perfume and an ominous hush.

"Well, that makes up my mind for me!" said Duncan, almost to himself.

"Don't take any notice of her!" said Oliver. "You've all been a huge help. Look how much food we all foraged the other day. The kids as well!"

"They eat a lot, though," Gwen said, sounding depressed. "And she's always complaining about the noise they make."

"No decisions until we hear from Des," Ellen reminded them, and George nodded his agreement. He leaned forward and patted Emily with one wing.

"Dry your tears, and listen for the Call," he said to her. "I feel in my bones that you have the gift as well. It is often passed down; Nan to Gwen, and maybe Gwen to you." Emily smiled at him. She resolved to work at it!

# Chapter 9

# Plan of Action

It was supper time before Des emerged from the tower and staggered down the stairs, yawning and bleary-eyed, but more like his usual self. Hearing him emerge, Angelica, jingling with jewellery, condescended to join the family for supper in the kitchen.

It was a splendid feast, and the children enjoyed Des's surprise when he saw it. When he had departed for Wales, the stocks of food had reached a low point, and the sight of barbecued pheasant, sticks of burnt and crunchy fish, rook rissoles and toasted fungus took him completely by surprise. The children kept interrupting each other as they told of the hunting and fishing expedition that had happened while he was away.

"Dad and I caught the fish. Can I have that last one, Mum?"

"Rook-hunting was brilliant, but pigeons taste better. We bagged lots."

"There's still some pheasants left. They're really slow and stupid. A fox nicked one from under our noses. I didn't know they could jump so high."

"We haven't eaten the rabbits yet either."

Des piled hot chillie sauce on his final rissole, crunched it whole and sat back with a satisfied sigh. "You kids are brilliant!" he said, accepting a mug of Firewater from Harold.

"Old enough to have some of that?" asked Ollie, hopefully as the jug was passed round.

"NO!" said the adults, in chorus. Des winked as he raised his mug. "Nice try, mate! Seriously, though, that was a fantastic day's work. I was getting worried that the food wasn't going to last. Aren't they a great bunch, Angie?" he added wickedly. Angelica gave a frosty smile. Everyone had noticed that she ate as heartily as anyone, even though she had done none of the hunting, plucking, cleaning or cooking!

"You'll want to talk things over and make some plans," said Maggie, who had enjoyed the feast as much as the others, even though she had done most of the cooking. "Let me put the wee ones to bed." She pretended to chase Georgie and Lily out of the room. Harold followed them.

A thoughtful silence descended. Des looked across at Duncan. "I gather your wing's holding up pretty well. Have you flown very far?"

"Not that far yet, but it feels fine. George, you did a great job patching me up! I'm sure I could manage the flight home if we waited for a spell of calm weather and took it in easy stages." Everyone looked at Gwen, who was frowning doubtfully.

"How's the thaw going, Des?" asked Ellen, changing the subject.

"There's still a lot of snow on the high hills, but it's melting down below. So now we've got Humans out and about again, which makes things trickier. You'd have to travel by night, to be on the safe side, but there aren't too many Human settlements between here and your Glen. We can avoid them. It'll take us longer, but that's no problem."

The young dragons looked at each other, all wondering the same thing, but deciding not to interrupt. It was rare that they were allowed at a grown-up conference and they didn't want to risk being sent away while decisions were being made.

"But what shall we do about Nan and Edward?" Gwen said. "That's the most important thing. Was Nan REALLY feeling stronger, Des, or were you just trying to make me feel better? I need to know!"

"Yes, she was a bit better, Gwen, truly. Before I left she came out and sat in the sun on the ledge outside their cave – you remember?" Gwen nodded, smiling. "But she's still weak. I had a long talk with Edward while she was sleeping and he had to agree that they were too old to stay alone for another winter."

"If ONLY we'd persuaded them to stay with us in the summer!" Gwen said to Duncan.

"We tried!"

"They seemed so well and strong then," said Ellen. "You couldn't know this would happen."

"I need to go and see them for myself!" Gwen sounded determined. Duncan sighed. He could see his hoped-for return to the Glen delayed.

Des held out his mug for more Firewater. "The obvious thing is for us to split forces," he suggested. "I'll take Gwen to Wales. If Nan's up to the journey, the four of us could travel up to the Glen together from there. That frees Duncan and the rest of you for travelling North from here whenever you decide the time is right."

"But what if they decide they want a last summer at home?" Gwen was still looking doubtful.

"I could go back and keep an eye on them for you."

"But you want to go Travelling!" Gwen protested.

"I owe Nan and Edward a lot," said Des. "I'd stay around for them. And you," he added.

"I could take the kids back to the Glen by myself, especially if we take it in easy stages," said Duncan.

"Tom and Emily yes – but what about Lily?" said Ellen. "She's not as big as Georgie, but she's getting quite a weight for a long distance." Duncan frowned, realising she was right, but not wanting to admit it.

"We could take her to Wales," Des suggested, but Gwen shook her head firmly.

"May I make a suggestion?" Angelica interrupted with her sweetest smile. "Why don't you leave darling

Lily here with me? There are plenty of us to look after her. Then when Gwen is home and your cave is ready, we can arrange to fly her back to you. I know that Des will be coming back here just as soon as he's sorted out all your problems." Ollie sniggered, but Alice nudged him into silence. Duncan was scowling again.

Ellen looked at Gwen. She was aware that her friend had always distrusted Angelica's fondness for Lily, but this idea was worth considering. "Yes," she said, "why not? Lily is used to us and loves Maggie. Duncan, you can't risk carrying her all that way. Tom and Emily should manage without help, but *they* couldn't carry Lily."

Ollie could keep quiet no longer. "Why can't we ALL go up to the Glen? We can all take turns carrying the kids. Problem solved!"

"Duncan doesn't want to wait until we're ready to go," said Oliver.

"We can be ready any time," Ollie started to argue, but Alice gave him a sharper nudge to shut him up.

"We're not sure of our plans yet. It's still too cold for camping in the open up North," Ellen said.

"The complication is me," Old George said calmly. "Gwen isn't the only one with a problem parent! I need to decide if I can travel to your Glen, or whether I should stay here with Angie."

"Father, we've decided already..." Angelica began, but George interrupted.

"*I* haven't," he said firmly. "When I do, I'll let you know. Just now, the problem is Nan, and Gwen and Duncan are the only ones who can decide what is best to do."

Emily was bursting with a new idea, and could keep quiet no longer. "Mum, could I go with you and Des to see the Gramps? PLEASE! I know I could fly as fast as you. I really want to see Gran!"

"She'd love to see you. She talked about you a lot," said Des. "I wouldn't mind taking you, Emily, but it's up to your Mum and Dad to decide."

"There's no need for any final decisions tonight," said Oliver firmly. "There's no way Des can start back to Wales without at least one decent night's sleep, and there's a lot of planning needed before any of us leave. I think you kids should head down to bed. And no sitting in a huddle hatching wild plans of your own down there! Are you listening, Ollie? We're all in this together."

"We understand," said Alice in her most grown-up voice. "Come on, you lot." She led the way out of the kitchen and the others followed reluctantly. Emily gave Des her most pleading look as she followed the others. He smiled sympathetically, but she knew he was right; it was for her parents to decide.

"What are we going to do?" Tom burst out as soon as they were safely in the cellar, but if he was expecting his hero Ollie to produce a 'wild plan', he was disappointed.

"Nothing we *can* do," he said. "They're right. We could leave here and camp somewhere like we usually do, but not up north for a while yet, and not with Grandad. We don't even know if the snow's melted up in your Glen. Obviously Duncan thinks it's worth risking. That's because old Ange insulted him this morning, of course. Des will go to Wales with your Mum, but I bet they won't risk taking you, Emily. It was a nice try though!"

"I think we're going to have to accept that our families might split up," Alice said sadly. "It's been great, being all together, even though we've been a bit bored stuck in here. But we don't KNOW we'll be coming to spend the summer in your Glen. Whatever the parents decide, it looks as though our time together is nearly over!"

# Chapter 10

# A Meeting by the Pond

Probably Desmond was the only dragon who slept soundly in the old house that night. He was still very tired, and he alone had no big decision to make. As soon as Gwen was ready to go to Wales, he would go too. Almost everyone else was either worried, undecided or, in the case of the four young dragons, frustrated because they were allowed no real say in the decision-making. Even Tom tossed and turned in his hay, brooding over the prospect of a summer without Ollie.

When the children emerged, rather late, they found Ellen and Gwen had already started planning, and were sorting through the stores deciding what could be spared for Nan and Edward, and how much Duncan could carry to the Glen. As soon as she saw

Emily, Gwen decided not to keep her in suspense, and drew her away from the others.

"Dad and I don't want you to come to Wales, and then all the way home, Emily. I know you fly well now, but it's a long way and a big risk for you to fly out over the sea. Des admits that's the only safe way to get to the Gramps from here. I'm sorry, love." She paused, seeing Emily's sad face and drooping wings. "I know you want to see Gran, but I'm hoping I can bring them up to live with us in Ben's cave, so you'll see lots of them then. Cheer up!"

"How long will you be away?" Emily asked, downcast.

"I don't know. But Des will come back with me, so you know I'll be safe. And you want to see Ben again, don't you? And the otters?"

"I want Alice too."

"I think they'll come up again later on. They all like our Glen. Go and have your breakfast, and don't worry. We'll not be leaving today."

"Hard luck," said Alice, seeing Emily's expression as she joined them.

"Thought so!" said Ollie. "They just won't accept that we're growing up."

"Shut up, Ollie, you're not helping," said Alice.

"And it's raining really hard!" said Tom gloomily.

In fact the rain proved a blessing. Later in the morning after Des had disappeared for a private recce, he persuaded the parents that it would be safe for him to take the four of them swimming in the large pond. "No sign of Humans anywhere. This rain should keep them away," he argued. "If there are any of their machines around, we'll hear them and have plenty of time to hide."

"We might catch some more fish," said Tom, delighted at the possibility of showing off.

"It would certainly be nice to have some peace," Angelica said pointedly. "How thoughtful of you, Desmond! I'll see you later." She bestowed a smile on him as she swept out of the kitchen to her favourite red couch. Des punched Ollie, who was whooping with glee, and then Tom, who was making loud sick noises, and swept the four of them outside.

"One more snigger, and we don't go!" he threatened, and the boys calmed down. Emily was surprised at how annoyed she felt when Angie flirted with Des, but forgot it in her pleasure at being outside with all her friends, even in the rain.

The trees of the wood grew close to the pond at one side, though on the other there was a wide area of grass and a Human track. The dragons went the roundabout way, through the trees, and Des made them stay under cover while he went out cautiously to check for Humans. The rain was still falling steadily. He came back to report that the place seemed deserted, but insisted that one of them stay to keep watch on the bank. He was taking no chances.

A large fallen tree right on the pond's edge provided a lookout post, and Des settled down on it while the four of them explored the pond. It was quite shallow, compared to the loch back in the Glen, and rather muddy, with reeds growing thickly round the edge. The water was freezing! Tom ran ahead and dived straight in, followed by Ollie. Alice and Emily paddled more cautiously round the edge before risking a swim. Even though Des was on guard, they kept a wary eye out for Humans. There were moorhens in the reeds, and two very noisy coots. Tom splashed out again clutching a flapping fish, which he presented to Des, and the girls laughed at his triumphant expression as he dived back into the water. "He does love being the best at something, doesn't he?" said Alice.

After a while, the girls decided to relieve Des of his watch on the log, and sent him to join the boys. "Listen hard as well," he reminded them.

"Don't risk one of your nose-dives!" Emily called as he left, and got a wave in response. "I wouldn't like him to get stuck in the mud," she said as they settled on the log. "Imagine all four of us having to haul him out by the tail!"

They had settled cheerfully into making optimistic plans for the summer ahead when they were violently interrupted. Without warning they heard a frenzy of barking and two black dogs raced to the water's edge. There was no time to warn the three dragons in the water, but Emily saw a flurry as all three dived and swam towards the thickest reeds. As she and Alice slid out of sight behind the log, she realised in horror that the dogs, after barking wildly on the bank, had splashed into the water and were swimming across. At the same time they heard Human shouts and running feet.

"Oh no!" moaned Alice, crouching down. "What are we going to do? We can't help the others. Shall we fly back by ourselves? I'm sure that's what Des would want us to do."

"Sssh! Wait! Listen," said Emily urgently. They held their breath, and heard a clear voice call "Tam, Toddy, come back! TAM!"

"No!!"Alice whispered in horror as she saw Emily very cautiously raise her head over the log. Then she heard her gasp of amazement. "It's Lisa! Honestly! Lisa and Finn! They're trying to call the dogs back. I don't think they've seen the others. They're probably hidden by the reeds."

"Any big Humans with them?"

"No. I'm going to let them see me!"

"You can't!" Alice gasped, but it was too late. Emily stood up on the log and waved her wings. She saw Finn shout and point at her, and Lisa stopped calling her dogs and stared too. One dog had swum back to shore, but the other was still in the middle of the pond, heading towards the hidden dragons in the reeds.

"Is it safe?" Emily shouted across the water, and both children nodded their heads. They started to run towards Emily. As they reached the edge, there was a rush of wings and Des, Ollie and Tom burst all together from their hiding place and hovered above the water, scattering drops. The dog in the water turned in terror and paddled furiously to join the children. Des let out a burst of flame and led the others to the log. Alice climbed up to join Emily.

Lisa and Finn stopped abruptly and looked ready to run. "Is it safe?" Lisa echoed Emily. "YES!" she called, confident that Des would not attack. As she watched, both dogs were fastened to leads, and the children walked slowly towards their log. Des nudged Ollie, who turned and scanned the open field, in case any other Humans appeared. The rain came down harder as the children and their dogs drew near and stopped, still a little wary of getting too close to Des.

Emily beamed. "It's lovely to see you again," she said.

"I never thought we would. I thought you had to stay hidden!" Finn said.

"We thought we'd be safe because it's raining so hard. We didn't think Humans would be out in the rain."

"We were bored and decided to take the dogs for a walk," said Lisa, moving a little nearer. "We usually bring them this way. We like the pond. It was frozen over a couple of weeks ago and was great for skating. It's a good thing you didn't come then. There were lots of people here."

"That's why we didn't come." It was the first time Des had spoken. "I knew all about the Humans here. You just didn't see me!" He still looked scowling and unfriendly, and was causing both dogs to cower behind the children.

"Why aren't you at school?" Emily asked.

Lisa looked astonished. "It's Sunday. How do you know about school?"

"We saw you and wee Charlie get off your School Bus!" said Emily, and then saw that Alice and Des were both looking at her open-mouthed. Ollie glared at her, and she realised her mistake.

Fortunately Tom distracted them. "Ollie and me really liked that football you left us. Tell Charlie we've played a lot," he said.

"And the books were lovely," Emily added. "We've read them all, haven't we Alice? That's how we learnt about your School place. Thank you!"

"Say thank you to Megan too," Alice added, relaxing a little.

"She'll be furious that she didn't come out with us," Finn said. "She's talked about you a lot."

"I KNEW it!" Des burst out.

"Oh, only to us!" Finn assured him hastily. "We've said nothing to any grown-ups. We kept our promise. And we've never been back to the old ruin after we left those things for you."

"Keep it that way!" said Des grimly. "Most of us are leaving in a day or two, but there'll still be plenty of big fire-breathers left, believe me. Get along home now, and keep your mouths shut – you and your dogs."

"We will. And the dogs can't talk!" said Lisa. "I'm SO glad we saw you again. We'll never forget you, will we, Finn. Goodbye, and stay safe!"

Both children turned to go, breaking into a run across to the track with the two dogs galloping alongside. At the edge of the field they turned and waved. Emily, Alice and Tom waved back enthusiastically.

"I hope she was right – dogs can't talk," said Ollie thoughtfully. "After all, we know foxes can."

"I think you and Emily might have a bit of explaining to do!" said Des ominously. "But we'd better get home ourselves, before any more Humans come snooping. That was enough danger for one day, even for me."

"It wasn't dangerous, it was magic!" said Emily happily as they retreated into the safety of the trees.

## Chapter 11

# Escape from the Castle

Four days later, many miles from the Castle, a weary Emily was trying to get to sleep. Although the sun was rising and she had buried herself in bracken, she wasn't really warm enough. A V-shaped skein of geese had just flown over, their honking cries reaching her even though they were flying high, and she had tried counting them, but it hadn't helped. If she didn't have a decent sleep, she'd never manage the flight tomorrow, but worrying about it was keeping her awake. She envied her father and Tom, who had both dropped off almost as soon as they had settled down.

She went over the happenings of the last few days in her head. As darkness had fallen the day after their secret encounter with Lisa and Finn, Gwen and Des had set off for Wales. It was obvious that Gwen hated leaving her family behind, but there was nothing else she could do. After hugs and promises that she would come home as soon as she could, she set off with Des, weaving through the woods and heading for the deserted moorland beyond.

As soon as they had departed, Duncan started making plans for the return to the Glen. Nothing that Oliver or Ellen could say would change his mind, though he did agree to Oliver flying with them for the first night, just to make sure that his mended wing would stand up to the long flight. And it had been agreed that Lily should remain with Ellen and Maggie until Gwen was back and they could arrange to bring her home.

It had been horrible saying goodbye to Alice and Ollie, but Emily had been a little comforted when Ellen, hugging her in farewell, had whispered that it wouldn't be long before they were back in their woodland camp. Lily hadn't understood what all the fuss was about, and had hidden under Angelica's couch and refused to come out to say goodbye. Emily hoped nobody had noticed the tears she had shed as she left her wee sister behind.

The first night flight had started out quite exciting, but both Tom and Emily soon wearied of the darkness. Fortunately there was only a light wind, and that was from the south, helping them along. They flew high, for fear of Singing Strings which had caused such disaster on their way to the castle, and saw few signs of Human habitation. As dawn was breaking they made their way into the shelter of a forest and slept in safety, glad to have the first flight over. While the children slept, Duncan and Oliver discussed the route ahead, and then Oliver left them to return to his family in the castle.

When they had woken in the early afternoon, they saw that the day was grey and overcast and Duncan decided they would be safe to start before nightfall. The rolling hills seemed empty of Humans, so there was little risk, and they could allow themselves a rest in the middle of the night. Duncan was proud of his children. They were keeping a steady pace without complaining. Tom had accepted one lift from Oliver on the first night, but since then he had flown by himself, obviously proud that at last he was being treated like a grown-up dragon.

Duncan had estimated that one more night's journeying would see them in sight of Ben and the welcome safety of their cave. Emily couldn't wait! If only she could get to sleep... She buried her head in the bracken and shut her eyes firmly. Tom and her father found it very difficult to wake her up for supper before they set out on the last leg of their long journey.

As they flew north, they saw that there were larger patches of snow, especially on the tops of the hills. Rivers were full and rushing down the valleys, and there were large pools of melt water trapped in hollows. It wasn't freezing any more, but it was still cold for the dragons as they kept up a steady pace through the drizzle, trying not to think of Gwen and Lily, their friends, their aching wings, hot food, and the comfort of the castle they had left behind.

Back at the castle, Lily was causing a headache for everybody. When Maggie had lured her out of her hiding place and tried to put her to bed with Georgie, she fought and huffed and refused to lie down. Eventually she fell asleep from sheer exhaustion, to everyone's relief. The grown-ups hoped that she would settle down and be her usual bouncy self after a night's sleep, but she spent the next day fighting with Georgie, refusing to eat and sulking when Alice tried her best to entertain her. Every suggestion was met with "NO!" At one point she escaped through the hole in the door and galloped across the garden. Fortunately Ollie managed to catch her before she reached the fence, and brought her back, squirming, lashing her tail and trying to fight her way free. Georgie watched from the top of the steps, obviously rather impressed.

On the second day Angelica decided to take over. This was her chance to fulfil a secret hope that she could persuade Lily to stay and live in the castle with her, instead of returning to the cave in the Glen. She had been obsessed with the rare golden dragon baby from the first sight back in Scotland. Now she tried to tempt her with beads, with a game of bouncing on her large bed, with her secret store of honeyed snails, and even with the precious jewellery in her handbag, but nothing would satisfy the angry little dragon. Eventually, after Lily had swiped her hard across the face with her spiky tail during her fourth tantrum of the afternoon, Angelica admitted defeat and handed her back to Ellen and Maggie. Perhaps even a *golden* baby was not quite the fashion accessory she was looking for!

"You can't blame the poor babe!" said Maggie fiercely when Angelica complained. "She doesn't understand why her Mum disappeared, and then the rest of her family went away too. Shall Maggie find a bramble biscuit, pet?" she asked fondly.

"Yes!" said Georgie, scampering up.

"NO!" said Lily.

The next morning, Alice burst into her parents' room. "Lily's gone!" she shouted.

"WHAT?"

"We can't find Lily! Georgie's still asleep and she's not with him. Maggie's in the kitchen and hasn't seen her. She sent Harold outside to look, and Ollie's searching the cellar, and I've looked up here in the room with the cupboard. She isn't with Grandad, or Auntie Ange..."

"She can't have disappeared! She'll be hiding somewhere. She'll come out for breakfast." Oliver, heading for the stairs, tried to be reassuring, but Ellen and Alice looked at each other, worried. They had learned to be wary of Lily's fierce determination these last few days, and there were plenty of hiding places in the old house.

"Wasp waffles with honey for breakfast!" Ellen announced loudly at the top of the stairs, and waited hopefully. Georgie bounded up happily and headed for the kitchen, but no small golden dragon appeared. "Save some for me," Alice said, and resumed her search. She was becoming more and more convinced that Lily had escaped outside to look for her mother. If so, she could be in real danger. She thought of Gwen in Wales, and the others flying home, none of them knowing that Lily had disappeared, and her eyes filled with tears.

"We'll find her, don't worry," Ollie's voice behind her sounded unusually sympathetic.

Alice sniffed. "I think she might have gone outside."

"So do I. She tried to escape the other day, remember? Quick breakfast, then we'll go and look for her."

Dawn was breaking when Duncan, Emily and Tom, flying slowly and wearily, caught a glimpse of Ben McIlwhinnie in the distance. They passed over the old castle site and headed up the Glen.

"Can you manage these last few miles?" Duncan asked, aware that both children had been struggling to keep their wings beating. "I could carry you one at a time. I don't want to hide up for another day if we can avoid it."

"I think I can make it," Emily panted.

"Climb on, Tom," said Duncan. "You've flown really well, but you need a rest." Tom was too tired to protest. They battled on slowly. It was good to see wide patches of grass and heather, but there was enough piled snow to make Emily worry that their cave might still be blocked by the mighty drift that had covered the gorse bush, and shut them in a few weeks ago. She was longing to feel safe and warm in her cosy bedroom.

They flew over the loch, noticing a rim of ice and patches floating in the open water. There was no sign of the otter family. Through the familiar woods they flew, and there in front of them was Ben, back on his seat, sleeping peacefully. And there was the gorse bush, free of snow, their fireplace swept clear and the cave ready to welcome them home.

Duncan and Emily collapsed, breathless, at Ben's feet and Tom slid to the ground.

"The big drift's gone!" he said. "I wonder why. There's still plenty of snow around."

"I reckon Ben cleared it away for us when he got back," Emily said and her father nodded agreement.

"Quick drink at the stream," he said. "Then a long sleep for both of you. I'll check around first. Don't fall in! The torrent's a lot fiercer than usual." He smiled proudly as he watched them stagger down the hill, and went into the cave. There were puddles on the floor, but the inner caves were dry and nothing seemed to have disturbed the remaining stores on the rock shelves, though they needed tidying after Des had grabbed a selection in a hurry. Good old Des! He hoped he would soon bring Gwen back home from Wales.

Tom and Emily paddled wearily in through the puddles.

"Shall we help to clear these?" asked Emily.

"They can wait 'til tomorrow. Your bracken beds are nice and dry. Have a good sleep!"

Emily gave her dad a hug. "It's LOVELY to be home!" she said, and disappeared into her cave. Tom flopped wearily onto his own bracken bed and yawned loudly.

Then he had a shock.

Two large, round, greenish-yellow eyes were staring fiercely at him from the darkness at the back of his cave!

## Chapter 12

# Search and Rescue

Everyone gathered in the kitchen for a hasty breakfast while they decided what to do. Eventually, Maggie, Harold and Angie, who knew the old house best, agreed to search every possible hiding place inside while the others tackled the garden and the old outbuildings. Ollie and Alice were still sure Lily had escaped into the wood. There was no sign of her in the garden, but the discovery of a small gap in the barrier Des had constructed to block the hole in the fence confirmed their suspicions. Lily *had* gone outside; and since nobody knew when she had disappeared, she could have travelled a long way. The parents eventually agreed they should all go out to search the undergrowth as thoroughly as they could.

"She'll be so frightened!" said Alice, close to tears.

"Not likely, knowing Lily!" said Oliver. "She may be small, but I've never seen her *really* frightened of anything! She just pretends. Don't worry. I'm sure she won't have come to any harm."

"What if she's been spotted by Humans?" asked Ellen.

"That could be a problem, I admit. She's too small to frighten *them*, but she might have been captured. She can't fly very well yet."

"They'd probably let her go again pretty quickly. A couple of her tantrums and they'd soon get fed up!" Ollie was trying to cheer Alice up, but could see that he wasn't succeeding. "Let's get going. We'd better split up."

"I'll see if I can pick up a trail at the hole in the fence," said Ellen and the others agreed, knowing how good a tracker she was.

"Don't go beyond the edge of the wood," Oliver added. "It won't help if any of us get spotted. No point trying to send a Huff, but give one long loud call if you find her."

Alice and Ollie nodded, and all four flew over the fence and disappeared into different parts of the wood. Ellen found few traces of the little dragon's pathway through the undergrowth. She was so small that she didn't break branches and brambles like the others did. She called Lily's name softly as she searched, but there was no answer. A small patch of flattened weeds gave her hope, but the hollow was cold and empty. She began to wonder how she would ever face her friend Gwen!

Ollie headed for Ben's Stone, hoping that Lily might have found a hiding place there, but there was no sign of her. He flew to the top and stood tall, hoping for a better view, but the wood was too thick to see far. He could hear a rustling in the grass and strained his ears, but then he heard a low call, and realised it was Alice. Obviously she hadn't found Lily either. Sighing, he scrambled down the rock and set off again. There was so much tangled undergrowth it seemed impossible to spot a small gold dragon who didn't want to be found!

Oliver headed for the river, reasoning that it might pose the greatest danger to a little dragon. The wood bore traces of Ben McIlwhinnie's arrival during the great snowstorm, in broken branches and trampled weeds and brambles. He stooped, looking for any traces of Lily, but there were no tracks that seemed to fit. He heard the river long before he reached it. The melting snow had swollen it into a brown rushing torrent. If Lily had come this way and fallen in, she might have been swept downstream and drowned. He tried not to think of that possibility, and made his way slowly upstream along the bank, calling as he went.

Alice was making her way even more slowly. She remembered that Lily was fond of climbing, so she kept stopping to scan the branches of trees above her, hoping to see a small gold shape looking down at her. Probably giggling! She also hoped to see one of the friendly hawks who had proved so helpful in the past, but there was no sign of them either. As she got further and further from the castle, with no sign of the truant she began to lose heart. She was straining her ears, hoping to hear the long call which would tell her that one of the others had found the wanderer, but there was nothing.

Suddenly she heard the distant barking of dogs, and froze. She knew that a dog usually meant that Humans were close by. Were they all in danger? What should she do? Her mind went back to the meeting with Lisa and Finn and their two black dogs. Could this be them? If it was, she could trust them, but how could she be sure?

As she crouched uncertain whether to go on or turn back, she heard a rustling behind her and whirled round. But it was only Ollie. She gave a sigh of relief. "Did you hear that?"

"Dogs, yes. That's why I headed this way. No sign of her anywhere back there."

"Could it be Lisa's dogs? Could they have found Lily? They might attack her!"

"Or she might attack them! Only one way to find out. Come on!" He squeezed past Alice and led the way cautiously in the direction of the barking. Alice followed closely. At times like these her irritating brother was a comfort! The sound grew louder.

Then they heard voices, confused and mingled with the barking, followed by the sound of running feet and snapping twigs, which grew fainter and then died away. Ollie picked up speed ahead of Alice, but stopped suddenly as he came out of the woodland and realised he had reached the edge of the road. He backed hastily and almost knocked Alice over.

"Did you see them? Was it Lisa?" she asked breathlessly.

"Couldn't tell. I thought I heard a girl's voice, but I couldn't be sure. Could be anyone. Might be nothing to do with Lily. It's a risk moving out into the open."

"What'll we do?"

Ollie thought for a moment. "We could keep under cover but head alongside this road-thing in that direction. That's the way they went, but I can't hear them now. If we see a Human we don't recognise, we'll just have to fly."

Alice nodded agreement, despite her misgivings, and followed Ollie as he wriggled into the cover of the bushes beside the road and crept along. Suddenly he stopped, and she moved alongside him. He was peering through a gap.

"What is it?" she whispered.

"That's their house. Emily and I saw Lisa and Charlie go in when they got off that Bus thing."

"It must have been their dogs we heard. Can we risk going to see?"

"Not both of us. I'd better go."

"No, I will," said Alice after a pause. "They were afraid of you but Lisa liked me. If I can find her it'll be OK. I can ask if they've seen Lily. You stay here and keep watch."

Ollie agreed reluctantly. "Perhaps you're right. I'll stay hidden. Yell if you need help. Good luck!"

Alice tried to smile bravely, which did not fool Ollie, and pushed her way through the long grass until she was directly opposite the house. Then she crouched with a beating heart, preparing to run across and fly over the gate into the unknown dangers of a Human garden. But before she could move, the gate opened and two figures came through. She held her breath and froze as she recognised Lisa and Megan.

The two girls stopped and looked up and down the road.

"They wouldn't be out in the open," she heard Lisa say.

"Let's go into the wood then," said Megan. "We must find them!"

"We'll head towards the ruin, and call as we go," Lisa decided. "Come on!" They crossed the road and headed for a track in the wood a few yards from where Alice was crouching. Then they stopped. "Emily! Alice! Are you there? Don't be frightened, it's only us!" Lisa called softly.

Very carefully, Alice emerged from her hiding place and both girls moved towards her. "Are you looking for something?" asked Lisa quietly.

"Because I think we've found it!" Megan opened her coat a fraction, and a small golden head poked its nose out.

"'Ello, Ally!" said Lily.

Alice let out a mighty huff of relief. "Wherever did you find her? We've been looking all over the wood!"

"We'll come in there and hide with you, just in case someone comes along," said Lisa, and the two girls crouched in the long grass beside Alice. "Is

Emily around? Is this the little sister she told me about?"

"Emily and Tom have flown home to Scotland with their Dad," Alice explained. "And their Mum's gone to Wales to see their Gran, who has been ill. Lily's staying with us for a bit. I expect she ran away to find them."

Lily's ears drooped. "Gone," she said sadly. Megan hugged her. "She is *so* cute!" she said. "I don't suppose I could keep her until they get back?"

"Of course you can't!" said Lisa.

"Where did you find her?"

"Tam and Toddy spotted her and started barking. She was sitting on the branch of a tree looking down, so they couldn't reach her. But she was frightened, so when we came up she jumped straight into Megan's arms! She snuggled under her coat quite happily. We had to get the dogs home, but then we thought we'd try and find one of you. We guessed you'd be looking for her."

"We're all out searching," said Alice. "She ran away in the night. We found her missing this morning. When we heard your dogs barking we guessed they might have seen her."

"Are the big fierce dragons out too?" Megan glanced round nervously.

"Only me!" Ollie moved out of hiding. The girls looked apprehensive. "Don't worry, I'm not going to attack! I trust you. Lily might have been seen by someone else if you hadn't found and hidden her. Thanks a lot! We'd better take her now. Climb on, Lily, and we'll get you home."

Megan opened her coat, and Lily emerged reluctantly. She gave first Megan and then Lisa a loving huff, scowled at Ollie and decided she would ride home with Alice instead.

"I expect this is the last time we'll see you," Alice said. "I think we'll be leaving the old house soon as well. We might be back next winter though."

"And we know where you live!" said Ollie with a grin. "That's not a threat this time, I promise. Come on, Alice, we'd better get this kid home and let the parents know she's safe." He turned to go.

"Thank you so much!" said Alice to the girls. "I'll tell Emily all about it when I see her."

"Give her our love," said Lisa.

"Bye, Lily. Don't run away again!" added Megan and Lily gave her a cheeky huff.

"And stay safe!" both girls chorused as Alice and Lily took off and followed Ollie into the trees. The wood echoed with the sound of his call as he sent the signal 'Found!' back to the castle. The two girls watched them disappear and then turned reluctantly for home.

## Chapter 13

# The Intruder

The eyes stared, unblinking. Tom's first impulse was to open his mouth and yell for his father, but then he remembered that he was now a grown-up, so he shut it again. Instead he sent a small flare to the ceiling, so that he could see who the eyes belonged to. By its light he saw a large striped cat, with ears flattened and teeth showing in a snarl. It had backed to the wall, but looked ready to pounce. Tom wondered what whether to run, but then, reasoning that teeth and claws wouldn't have much effect on dragon-hide, he stood his ground.

"What are you doing in my bedroom?" he hissed in a loud whisper. "Who are you?"

"Katt!!" the creature hissed back.

"Wild Cat?"

"Yess!!"

"I suppose you came in to shelter from the snow?"

"Yess!!"

"Well, OK, but it's our cave, and we're back now; Dad, Emily and me. I think you should go before Dad sees you."

"No. Musst sstay!" the cat hissed, flattening itself further against the wall.

Tom was too tired to argue. "Well, OK, just for today," he said. "You sleep over there. This is my bed. No attacking me while I'm asleep."

The cat blinked its yellow eyes. "Yess!" it hissed. Tom was too tired to care what it meant by that; he fell onto his bracken bed and was asleep almost at once.

The three exhausted dragons slept until late afternoon, woke for a quick meal, swept out the worst of the puddles and went back to bed, so Tom had no chance to say anything about his surprise visitor. In fact the cat had disappeared when he got up for supper, and he began to think he had dreamt the whole thing. But when he woke early the next morning, he saw that the cat was back, curled up asleep at the rear of the cave. He tiptoed out, wondering what to do. No-one else was awake.

Tom was worried. He was sure that Emily wouldn't mind a Wildcat sharing their cave, but he had a strong feeling that his father would object. Wildcats are very rare in Scotland. Tom had never met one before, but he knew they had a reputation as fierce and dangerous killers. Obviously they wouldn't be dangerous to dragons, he reasoned, but Dad would think that Lily might be frightened, when she came back. And the cat seemed determined to stay, for some reason. Sighing heavily, he went down to the stream for a drink, hoping that Dad or Emily would wake soon and make him some breakfast.

He was in luck. Emily was coming out of the cave as he returned. She was beaming at him. "Isn't it WONDERFUL to be back!" she said, standing with arms and wings outstretched and gazing down the Glen. "And the sun's shining!"

"It's still pretty cold," said Tom. "The stream's freezing, and we've quite a few snowdrifts left."

Should he tell Emily about Katt? He had almost decided to say something when his father appeared, yawning.

"That's better," he said. "Sun's shining and we've all had a decent sleep. Breakfast first, then we'd better get the cave swept and cleaned up before your mother gets home. And we need to replenish the stores. I wonder if that rabbit we left outside in the snowdrift is still there." It wasn't. Tom had a very good idea where it had gone!

"When will Mum get here?" asked Emily.

"No idea, but she and Des will fly faster than we managed, so could be any time. Tom, you get the fire going while we find something to eat."

It was a large breakfast, and Tom didn't want to spoil it by confessing about his unexpected lodger. But when all three of them were full and reluctantly thinking of starting on the day's chores, he felt he could delay no longer.

"Dad..." he started.

"Yes?"

"Er... there was someone in my room when we got home..."

"What? What sort of someone? Not another dragon?"

"No, it's... it's a Wildcat."

"WHAT!!"

"Wow!" said Emily. "I've never met a Wildcat. Is it still there? Can I go and see?"

"Tom, you're not telling me it's still *in* there? Didn't you get rid of it? Why didn't you call me?"

"It didn't want to go. I didn't want to force it out! It couldn't have known it was my bedroom. It was only sheltering from the snow. Honestly, Dad, it isn't doing any harm."

"They're fierce, you know. It could have gouged your eyes while you were asleep!"

"Well it didn't! It's called Katt, and I'm not afraid of it!"

Duncan gave an impatient snort, with more than a hint of flame, and strode into the cave. A few seconds later, a spitting, striped ball of fury, its fur and tail fluffed up so that it looked twice its usual size, dashed out of the cave, leapt onto Ben McIlwhinnie's right boot and turned to snarl at the dragons.

"See!" said Duncan, standing in the cave doorway with wings outstretched. "It's savage!"

"Katt!" Tom cried. "Don't run away!"

"Honestly, Dad, there's no need to drive it out like that!" said Emily, horrified. "You know what it was like in the blizzard. How could it have known this cave was ours? Don't be mean!"

Duncan's huffs subsided in the face of his children's combined disapproval, and the cat, sensing it, let its fur subside a little as it crouched on the boot.

"Well what am I supposed to do?" asked Duncan, exasperated. "It can't stay here now we're back!"

Tom was about to argue that he didn't mind sharing his bedroom when Emily gave a loud yell, which startled them all. "Look!" she shouted pointing at the sky. "It's Mum! And Des! They're nearly home!"

The three dragons turned to gaze down the valley and the cat took its chance, jumped down from Ben's boot and disappeared.

The flying dragons came nearer and nearer, while Tom and Emily danced with excitement. Duncan, relieved to see the cat depart, took off and flew to meet them. Then, with a flurry, all three landed between Ben's boots and the children rushed to hug their mother. "No Gramps?" asked Emily, as Tom and Des exchanged High Fours, both talking at once, and Duncan rushed down to the stream to fetch water for the travellers.

Gwen smiled wearily. "They couldn't come, Emily. Gran was a bit better by the time we left, but she isn't fit enough for such a long flight. I'll tell you more later. Tell me about *your* journey. When did you get back?"

Over steaming mugs of nettle tea and more break-fast, they swapped stories of their journeys. Duncan assured Gwen that his wing had held up well; Emily and Tom were quite embarrassed by their father's glowing account of their flying skills; Gwen told about flying over the sea, which she had never done before; and Des described their journey back from Wales, risking daytime travel by flying too high for Humans to see them. "Though I do hate flying in clouds. It's so boring! I like to see where I'm going!" Finally Emily assured her mother that Lily was fine, choosing not to tell of Lily's hiding and huffing as they left.

Just as Duncan was starting to confess that they hadn't done any foraging or tidying of the cave since they returned, Tom decided he could wait no longer. He burst out with his story of the Wildcat. "Where's it gone?" he said, flying up to Ben's boot and peering over the far edge. "Dad, you scared it away! It's not fair. I wanted it to stay."

"At least you got to talk to it. I didn't even have the chance!" said Emily. Gwen looked from one to the other and was about to ask questions, when Des pointed up to the ledge of Ben McIlwhinnie's knees. "There's your cat! However did it get up there?"

"Huh, cats can climb anything!" said Duncan, grumpily.

Gwen stood up and gazed up at the cat outlined against the sky. "You didn't turn her out?" she said, rounding on Duncan. "How could you? Obviously she'll have to stay for a while."

"Why?"

"Use your eyes! She's about to produce kittens. She needs a safe place to have them. She'd better have the Bone Cave. I'll go and fetch her down. Honestly,

Duncan...!!" She got up wearily and prepared to fly up to the ledge, but Tom scrambled to his feet.

"I'll go, Mum. She's not afraid of me. She can stay in my cave." He flew up to the cat, who crouched but did not run away. They couldn't hear the conversation, but it was obvious that Tom was coaxing her down.

Gwen raised her eyebrows. "Our boy's growing up!" she said, watching him. Duncan was scowling but Des chuckled and shook his head in admiration. "Good thing we got back when we did, Gwen," he said. "Tom and Duncan might have come to blows over that cat!"

Emily beamed. "Lily will LOVE playing with kittens," she said happily.

Duncan realised he was outnumbered. "OK, OK! Just don't blame me when it all goes wrong! We need some fresh food. I'm going fishing while you two catch up on some sleep. The kids can tidy up in there, can't they?" He took off before anyone could argue as Tom returned with Katt.

"In the Bone Cave you said?" said Des dubiously to Gwen, as the cat snarled and spat at him in passing.

"No, she's going back in my room," said Tom, disappearing with his new friend.

"Good!" said Des. "Bone Cave for me. See you later, Emily!"

Gwen smiled at Emily. "Make sure Tom does his share," she said, as she too headed for her bed. Left alone, Emily heaved a heavy sigh and wondered where to start.

## Chapter 14
# A Firelight Conference

The travellers emerged in time for a late supper, feeling much better. There was plenty of crispy fish, as Tom had joined his father at the loch when his share of the tidying had been done, more or less, and Emily had found some hot chillie dip when sorting the shelves. Afterwards they crunched beechnuts from the stores, and finished with steaming mint tea.

It was a cold clear night, with a thin new moon and a sky full of stars, and their fire glowed brightly and sent twists of smoke into the night.

"Great supper!" said Des, through a mouthful of nuts.

"There would have been more if Tom hadn't insisted on giving one of his fish to that wretched cat!" said Duncan.

"Never mind the cat!" said Gwen. "It's time we told you more about Nan and Edward, and made some plans. We need to get Lily back. I'm missing her."

"She'll be fine! You know how she loves Maggie and the others," said Duncan, but Emily was not so sure. She had a feeling that Lily wasn't happy, that something was wrong. Suddenly she wondered if this was a Call, but Gwen was starting to speak again, so she decided to think about it later, alone in bed.

"Nan is dying," said Gwen, leaning forward and speaking softly and sadly. "She knows. She's quite calm about it. She says it's nearly time, and it will happen soon. Edward realises too. He's a lot more vigorous than Nan. He can look after her. He insist- ed that we came home, and that Des should come with me. When the time comes she will Call. And when the Call comes, she wants Des to take Emily to Wales to say goodbye."

There was a shocked silence round the fire. Silent tears rolled down noses. Emily was the first to speak.

"Will you come too?" she asked her mother.

"I have said goodbye to her," Gwen said quietly. "She sent her love to Duncan, Tom and Lily, but she knows we can't all go to Wales safely, and she wants you, Emily. Will you go?"

"Of course I will!" said Emily, sniffing away tears. "Can't we go straight away? What if...."

"Wait for the Call," her mother insisted. "I'll hear it and I think you will too. Nan was sure you had the gift."

"She made me promise to take good care of Emily, and I will," said Des. He was looking unusually solemn. Tom was subdued too, and was not making his usual loud complaint that he was being left out of an adventure with Des, and it wasn't fair.

"How soon?" asked Duncan, who seemed to have accepted the plan without argument, to Emily's surprise.

"Not straight away," said Des. "She was stronger when we left, as we told you. She thinks she has a few weeks left, maybe longer. She's prepared for it. She will send the Call to Old George too, so the others will know."

There was silence round the fire as they thought of wise and kindly Nan, whom they all loved. Emily remembered their last talk on the beach in the summer, when she and Nan had crept away from the others and sat on the rock watching the sun set over the bay. Nan had spoken of her travelling to Wales, but she had never thought it would be so soon, or to say goodbye. She felt tears trickling down her nose again, and tried to swallow her sobs.

It was Gwen who broke the sad silence. "There are other things to think of as well," she said. "We have plenty to do while we wait for the Call. We need to bring Lily home. How can we manage that?"

"I'll go and fetch her!" said Des at once. "She'd be OK travelling with me, wouldn't she?"

"Of course she would," said Emily at once. "You're her big hero. She'd be thrilled!"

"Des, it's more than good of you to offer," said Duncan seriously. "But you can't keep flying round the country sorting out our problems. You've taken four long flights already for this family, and another journey is planned with Emily. You risked your life to rescue us all in the blizzard. You can't go all the way to the castle and back just for Lily!"

"It's not that far!" Des protested. "A few long flights will do me good. I was getting fat on Maggie's cooking and not getting nearly enough exercise in the castle."

"You have your own life to lead. You're a Traveller, remember?" said Gwen.

There was a long silence. The darkness had deepened, and the fire was dying down. It was difficult to see faces in the dimness. Emily held her breath. She had a feeling that something important was about to be voiced.

"Yes, I am a Traveller," Des said softly. "And I won't stop travelling, not yet. I think there's a good deal of the world left to explore. But I don't want to go back to being a *lonely* traveller, with no place to call home. My parents are dead. I've no family of my own. I sort of feel you've adopted me – you and the others down south. You say I've helped you, Duncan, and perhaps I have. But you've been good to me too. So, I'll look after Emily on the journey to Wales and back, and bring Lily safely home for you – agreed?"

There was another pause. Gwen looked at Duncan, who squeezed her talon and smiled. "Agreed! Thank you."

Des got up. "No worries!" he said, with an obvious attempt to sound like his usual carefree self. "Better catch up on some more sleep before I go!" He disappeared into the cave, leaving the family feeling rather stunned.

"Bed for you as well," Gwen said to her children, after a pause, while they listened to Des crashing around in the Bone Cave before he settled down.

Emily gave both her parents a hug. "Thank you for letting me go to see Gran. I'll be quite safe with Des. And it will be lovely to have Lily back. I'm missing her too."

"Sleep well!" said her mother. "Don't lie awake grieving for Nan. She wouldn't want you to do that."

"I'm going to practise the Call!" said Emily, going into the cave. Tom followed her, unusually subdued. "I'm sorry you're not coming with us," she added as they reached their private caves.

Tom tried to sound nonchalant, even though he was secretly disappointed. "That's OK. I've got Katt to look after. I'm a bit worried about Des, though. I've never heard him talk like that before. Do you think he's getting old, like Ollie said?"

"Of course he isn't!"

"Just as well," said Tom. "For one awful minute I thought he was going to say he was planning to settle down at the castle with Old Ange!"

## Chapter 15

# The Otters Return

When Emily and Tom emerged for breakfast the following morning, they discovered that Des had already left for the castle.

"He's not flying in daylight is he?" Tom asked through a mouthful of porridge.

"Yes, he reckons it's safe enough if he's on his own," Duncan answered, passing Emily her breakfast. "He knows the best route to take to avoid Humans, and it's probably still too cold for many of them to be out and about. There was a frost again last night, so Gwen's off gathering firewood. I think we need to rebuild our stock. Plenty of stick-jumping for you, Tom!" He took off from Ben's left boot and headed for the woods beyond the swollen stream.

"I wonder when the otters will come back to the loch," Emily said. "They did say they'd be back when the ice is off the water, and it's nearly gone. It's odd not to have Lottie and Wattie down there."

"No more tail-stane on the ice," said Tom, sadly. "I did bring one of those tennis balls back though, so we might be able to play on the grass like we did at the castle."

"Not much point trying to play round here," said Emily. "The ball would just roll down the hill!" Tom didn't reply. He was trying to think of a good flat place suitable for introducing the otters to his new version of their game.

"Is the cat still there?" Emily asked, taking advantage of their father's absence.

Tom nodded with his mouth full. "Yes. I think her kittens will be born soon. She's made a soft nest with some of my bracken and her own fur. I'm going to move into the Bone Cave to give her some peace."

"Really? Will there be enough room for you?" Emily was astonished. Her little brother was being surprisingly thoughtful!

"Course! I can squeeze in with the firewood. Don't say anything to the parents yet," he added as they saw Gwen flying slowly towards them with a load of branches. "I'll jump them!" he called as she landed. Gwen left the pile for him and came to Emily, who was still finishing her breakfast.

"You know that Des has gone, I suppose?" she said, sitting next to Emily and warming her talons by the fire.

"Yes, Dad said. Lily will be really proud, flying home with Des. She'll feel like a big grown-up dragon. I bet she makes a fuss about travelling in a sling, though."

"Ellen has worked out ways of carrying Georgie safely," Gwen answered. "She'll make sure Des knows what to do. And Lily is much more likely to behave for Des."

"I have a feeling she's missing us," said Emily thoughtfully. "I keep thinking about her. Do you think she might be sending me a message? Perhaps she can do the Call as well."

"She's a bit young for that! I just hope she's not having too many tantrums. If she is, Ellen and Maggie will be very glad to see her go!"

"Old Ange might as well," said Emily. "I was always worried that Angie might kidnap her. She kept going on and on about 'darling Lily' and how rare golden dragons are. Now that Lily has become so bolshie, I think she'll change her mind about her!"

"I'm not worried about that any more. I know the others will make sure Lily comes home safely. And I'm sure Angelica won't want to come too."

"But if Des is coming she might change her mind..." Emily hinted.

Her mother chuckled. "Even with Des around, she won't want to come. After all, she thinks it snows all year round in Scotland! I think Des is safe, don't worry! He'll be relieved not to have Ollie sniggering all the time. I saw a patch of burdock when I was collecting the wood," she added. "Shall we fly down and see if we can dig up some roots? Dad and Tom can manage the wood."

For the rest of the day, the dragon family worked hard at replenishing the depleted winter stores. As the last snowdrifts melted, more frozen rabbits appeared and once the crows had been driven away, these were carefully collected and brought back to the cave. Tom volunteered to skin a couple for supper, and was able to sneak some of the raw meat to Katt in the process, to Emily's amusement. She saw the cat slink out of the cave to drink at the stream, but for most of the day she stayed hidden in Tom's room. She was not even tempted out by the smell of rabbit cooking on their evening fire.

The next morning was cloudy but a good deal warmer, and Duncan decided it would be good for fishing. He had also remembered that Oliver had told him that the roots of bulrushes could be roasted and eaten, when there were no stolen tatties available, and there were plenty growing round the fringes of the loch. He took Tom down with him, but Emily, who was a lot less keen on cold water, elected to stay behind. She took the opportunity to creep very carefully into Tom's cave to see Katt, and was pleased that the Wildcat accepted her offering of leftover rabbit, and did not snarl or hiss at her once. She had snuggled into a deep nest, and shook her head when Emily asked if she needed anything else. "Are you sure you're all right?" Emily asked anxiously, and was rewarded with the one word, "Yess." So Tom was not the only one Katt would talk to!

She was about to leave the cat in peace when there was a yell from outside. Katt flattened herself in her nest, but Emily hurried out, calling "Don't worry, it's only Tom!" over her shoulder as she left.

She found Tom dancing with excitement on Ben's left boot. "The otters are back!" he announced as soon as Emily appeared. "Coming down?" Emily agreed cheerfully, and they raced each other down to the loch. Emily won by a nose.

Duncan had retreated to the far end of the loch because the four otters had become a cheerful tumbling whirlpool in the middle. But when they spotted Tom and Emily, the two youngsters, now as big as their parents, dived, swam over and surfaced close to the dragons' rock.

"It's braw bein' back in deep watter!" Wattie exclaimed. "A river's no' bad, but ye keep bumpin' yer neb on the bottom!"

"Aye, an' muckle great rocks get in yer way! Did youse lot see oot the winter in yon cave?" Lottie called. The dragons started to explain about the snowdrift that had shut them in, and how they had gone south for the rest of the winter. The young otters were so interested that they climbed out onto the rock while they listened to the whole story of the blizzard, Duncan's accident and how Ben McIlwhinnie had been wakened by Des to carry them to the safely of the ruined house in the wood.

"Is Des no' back here?" asked Wattie.

"You couldn't have a ride even if he was," said Tom. "You're too big."

"Aye, pity that," sighed Wattie. "I fair enjoyed flyin' o'er the loch and fallin' in!"

"Where's yer wee bairn?" asked Lottie, and Emily explained that she was being brought home from the castle by Des. "She's grown a bit, and she's really bolshie. I hope she doesn't give him too much trouble."

"Ice's melted, so nae mair Tail-Stane!" said Wattie regretfully to Tom, but that gave Tom the chance he had been waiting for. Eagerly he began to tell the otters about the finding of the balls that the Humans had left in the castle, and how you could play a version of Tail-Stane on dry land. Emily was only half listening – she had heard it all before – but suddenly she realised that Tom was about to mention young Charlie and their other Human friends.

"Tom, it's a secret!" she exclaimed, but it was too late. At the same time, Lottie cried, "Ye've niver bin bletherin' wi' Humans?" She sighed and gave Tom a punch to shut him up.

"It's a deadly secret!" she said "You mustn't tell your parents, or ours. We'll get into dreadful trouble if they find out."

"Does Des ken aboot it?" asked Wattie.

Emily nodded. "He saw them too. But he won't tell."

"Ah dinnae think Humans're that bad," said Lottie. "We saw some at the Big River. They jist spied us and got dead excited. They didn'ae try tae kill us or chase us at a'!"

"Humans are nae problem," said Wattie scornfully. "They cannae swim and they cannae fly!"

"Ours were really nice," said Emily wistfully. "We were friends. But remember – the parents mustn't know!"

"We'll no' tell," Lottie promised.

At that moment there was a loud call from the other bank, and Lottie and Wattie looked across and announced they had to go. They slid into the water. "Try oot that geme the morn, aye?" Wattie yelled to Tom as he left and Tom gave a claws-up in reply. "Great!" he said. "That flat bit of the bank will be just right."

"You'd keep losing the ball in the water. And you haven't got another." Emily was less enthusiastic about the continuation of Tail-Stane.

"The otters could always get it back. Nae bother, as they say!" Without waiting for an answer, Tom took off and headed towards his father at the head of the loch. He hoped he might get a chance to do some deep-dive fishing himself.

Emily carried on sitting on the rock, stirring the water moodily with her tail. It was obvious that Tail-Stane in all its versions would continue to be Tom's great obsession. Sometimes he seemed to be growing up, but then he went back to being her annoying wee brother. She lapsed into a dream of Lisa, Megan and Finn. She was so far away that she jumped in shock as Duncan, three small fish in one talon, soared past her, grabbed a bunch of bulrushes growing beside her rock and yanked them out of the water with his other talon before heading up the mountain with his haul. Tom cheered and followed, carrying the rest of the fish. Emily, spattered with mud and water from the dripping bulrushes, scowled and sighed. Perhaps life back in the castle hadn't been so bad after all. She was really missing Alice!

# Chapter 16

# Cats and Caves

Emily's bad mood lasted the rest of the day. Everything was going wrong! Lottie and Wattie had seen her spattered with mud, and laughed at her. She did not enjoy the freezing plunge in the loch to get rid of the mud, or the flight back with wings too wet to work properly. The fire had gone out when she got back to the cave, so she couldn't get warm again. Tom went on and on about fishing and tail-stane until she felt like drowning him in the swollen stream. She retreated to the top of Ben's head, slightly comforted by the faint warmth she could feel through her talons, and gazed south, willing Des to appear with Lily, and longing for Ellen and Oliver to decide it was warm enough for outdoor living, even in Scotland. At least they had promised to come, eventually! But what if they changed their minds?

She didn't dare to think about her Gran, in case it made her cry again. And then Tom would jeer, and tell the otters, and they'd all laugh at her. Her mother, who usually understood, had flown into the woods by the smaller loch to search for berries and obviously wanted to be alone. If only Ben would wake, and give her someone sympathetic to talk to!

There were roasted bulrush roots for supper, to go with the fish, but Emily declared she hated their chewy, stringy texture and complained that they were not nearly as nice as tatties. Tom said he quite liked them, which annoyed her even more, and when her father said, with satisfaction, that there were so many bulrushes round the two lochs that they need never starve again, she burst into furious tears and stomped off to bed.

"What's the matter with *her*?" asked Tom in surprise, and even Duncan looked bemused.

"Life!" said Gwen. "She'll probably feel better in the morning. But perhaps lay off the bulrushes for a bit!" she added and flew down to the stream for a drink, leaving Duncan and Tom to shake their heads at each other, baffled by the mysterious workings in the minds of female dragons.

The next morning Emily did feel better, soothed by a few chapters of her favourite book when she woke early after a more restful night. She was up before Tom, but very soon he burst out of his temporary bedroom in the Bone Cave to announce important news.

"Katt had her kittens in the night!" he yelled as he came out. "Three of them. Tiny wee things, all squirmy. She wouldn't let me get near them, though."

"Then she needs peace and quiet, so stop shouting!" his mother said severely. "You must leave her alone. I'll go in and see if she needs anything in a few minutes."

"It's me she likes!" Tom protested.

"Oh, she's quite happy with me," Gwen assured him. "We've had several conversations while you've been away fishing. And she's spoken to Emily too.

But she won't like *any* of us if we disturb her kittens. Leave her to me for a day or two, then we'll see."

"I'm keeping well out of the way!" said Duncan, as the end of Gwen's tail disappeared into the cave. "Nothing more savage than a Wildcat with kittens to defend. They'll attack anything that moves." Tom huffed sceptically, but Duncan ignored him. "The important thing is that Lily mustn't know," he continued. "She'll be back soon, and the last thing we want is for her to rush in and get herself injured. That cat could do damage to a dragon as small as Lily. So no mention of kittens, do you hear me, Tom?"

Tom rolled his eyes. "All right, if you say so. But Katt won't attack Lily if I ask her not to."

"And how will we keep her out of Tom's cave anyway?" asked Emily, who also thought her father was making too much fuss. "The best way of making sure she *does* go in is to tell her she mustn't. You know what she's like!"

"We'll face that when she gets here." Duncan was feeling himself outnumbered again so he closed the argument by flying down to the stream to wash breakfast off his scales.

"Coming down to the loch?" Tom asked. "Wattie wants to try tail-stane with my tennis ball. It'll be much better if we all play."

Emily sighed. "I suppose so," she said without enthusiasm, but at that moment Duncan came back from the stream and Gwen emerged from the cave.

"Katt and the kittens are fine," she said. "But let's leave them in peace for today. If you and Tom go down for some Tail-Stane with the otters, Duncan, I think I'll do some exploring further up the mountain. I'd like to follow our stream to its source. It looks as though there might be a rocky valley up there, and you never know, I could even find another cave. Do you want to come with me, Emily?"

"Yes please!" said Emily, feeling more cheerful at once.

"Take a bag in case you find some food up there," Duncan suggested.

"We might eat it all ourselves on the way home!" said Gwen.

"You don't think Des and Lily will come while we're away?" Emily suggested as they set off. "It would be awful if they flew all that way and found nobody at home."

"They're almost certain to pass over the loch, so the others will see them. But we could send a Huff from higher up. They might well be in Huff range now. It depends how long Des needed to stay at the castle before he set off. He might have decided to rest up for a few days. Maggie's cooking is worth staying for, even if he has to put up with Angie as well."

"I bet they all try to persuade him to stay," said Emily, rather despondently. "And what if the Call comes from Gran and he's still not back?"

"Oh, he'll be here before the Call comes! I have a feeling he's already on his way. Look, lots of rowan trees up ahead. Let's see if there are any berries left."

They left the stream and flew to a small copse of leaning trees, clinging to the rocky ground. Sure enough, they found a few berries left by the birds, wrinkled but still sweet and tasty. "Not enough to take home!" they agreed, eating quite a lot and saving a few to eat further up the mountain. There were more pockets of snow up here, the remnants of the deep drifts of winter which, if the sun never reached them, might stay all summer. Two mountain hares, looking odd with their coats half winter-white and half the brown of summer, took fright and shot away as the dragons flew low over their heads.

By now the stream was smaller, though still swollen with melting snow, and it wound between large rocks and hurtled fast downhill. A little further on they came to a waterfall, which reminded them both of Des, and his fondness for flying through them. "Though even Des wouldn't try that one," Gwen remarked. "There are far too many rocks in the way."

They flew to the top and found themselves in a gorge with steep rocky sides. On their way up the middle, they came to a rock so large that the stream had to detour round it. It made a good vantage point, so Gwen and Emily landed and scanned the rocky walls on either side for any signs of a cave.

"Up there!" Emily pointed. "That looks like one. That dark shape in the rock. Shall I fly up and see?" Gwen nodded, so she soared up to the rock wall, feeling like a real explorer. When she reached it she was disappointed. It was a tall cleft, but didn't seem to go back very far. She managed to land on the edge, which was tricky but possible and crept into the cave. Sure enough, it was too shallow to give much shelter. She came out again and shook her head at her mother, who pointed further up the gorge with one wing. Flying in that direction, Emily soon saw what her mother had spotted; another dark shape, a little higher up.

This one was much more like a proper cave, and Emily waved her mother up to join her once she had landed. It was lower but deeper, a single chamber without the inner rooms that she like so much in Ben's cave. It had a small rocky ledge at the entrance, just big enough to land on. "This could be made quite cosy," Gwen said, thoughtfully.

"It's not as nice as ours. Why do we need another one?"

"Oh, you never know!" said her mother, vaguely. "It might come in useful. Noisy neighbours, though!" she added as a pair of ravens, cawing harshly, flew right past them and landed on an untidy nest of sticks further along the rock wall.

"If we fly to the top we might be high enough to send a Huff to Des," Emily reminded her, and Gwen agreed. For some reason that Emily didn't understand, she seemed to have found what she was looking for.

The top of the hill proved a good Huff point, with a wide view to the south, and both dragons joined to send the Huff. To their delight a distant answer came back; *nearly home*

"Oh no!" Emily cried. "I want to be there when they land!"

"We'll make it, I think. Come on, we'll be able to fly faster than Des, after his long journey."

They took off together and sped along the gorge and down the mountainside, following the stream. It was an exhilarating race! When the domed shape of Ben's head came in sight, they saw that Tom was already jumping up and down with excitement on the top. "You join him! It looks as though they're in sight," Gwen said, a little breathlessly, and flew down to the ledge below, where Duncan was standing, also gazing south. In the distance they could see

Des flying slowly towards them, and as he got nearer, make out the small shape of Lily, sitting on his back and waving wildly.

"She isn't holding on! She'll fall!" Emily gasped, but Lily didn't. Des made a wide circle round Ben's head, while the young dragons waved and cheered, and then came to land on his right boot. Emily, watching from above, realised that her little sister was safely tied on with a bright red harness, and as they landed to join the others, Gwen was freeing her and lifting her down.

"'Ello, Emly!" Lily called triumphantly. "Des'n'me flew all'a way."

# Chapter 17

# Lily Causes Trouble

The fish supper was late but was worth waiting for. Maggie had sent everyone a present of bramble biscuits, which took the edge off their hunger, and Emily shared the remaining rowan berries with Tom and Lily. Tom was very scornful of their foraging up the mountain, so Emily decided not to tell him about the cave in the gorge. Between them they kept Lily away from the cave and the hidden Wildcat family by taking her to play by the stream, while Des sat recovering from the flight with a mug of nettle beer, roasting some tatties which he had carried with him at the bottom of Lily's sling, and giving Duncan and Gwen an account of the flight.

When they had finished the leisurely meal, Gwen decided it was well past Lily's bedtime. "No!" said

Lily cheekily, running away and hiding behind Ben's right boot. Duncan's offer of a ride on his back into the cave, Tom's attempt to chase her in, and Emily's bribe of a bedtime story were all met with the same response, increasing in volume. Finally Des got up, rather wearily. "You'll come with *me*, won't you, Lily?" he coaxed. Lily stopped stamping her feet and treated him to her very best wide-eyed gaze. Everyone waited hopefully while she batted her eyelashes.

"No!" she said firmly, smiling sweetly at him.

At this point, Gwen tucked her under one arm and carried her, lashing her tail and protesting loudly, into the cave.

Tom sighed. "I hope Katt doesn't come out to see what all the noise is about," he said. "She's got three kittens, Des, so she's supposed to be getting some peace and quiet. Fat chance now Lily's back!"

"Lily had a bit of an adventure back at the castle," said Des. "When Gwen comes back I'll tell you about it." He stretched and yawned. "She was remarkably good on the flight, though she objected to the sling unless she was really sleepy." He closed his eyes as Tom embarked on a detailed account of re-invented

Tail-Stane with the otters. Emily sympathised! She decided she preferred telling Lily the promised bed-time story.

A good deal later, with Lily finally asleep and Des awake again, the story of Lily's escapades was told to the rest of the family. Gwen was horrified to hear of her tantrums and general bolshieness, and was obviously feeling thoroughly guilty about leaving her with Maggie and Ellen. Even Duncan's point that it would have put Angie off Lily for good didn't really cheer her up. Tom and Emily thought the whole story was funny. But when Des told them that Lily had escaped into the wood and was missing for a night and most of a day, they were horrified.

"There was a search party out. Oliver and Ellen AND Alice and Ollie! Eventually it was Alice who found her. Fortunately she remembered that Lily loved climbing, so she looked UP for her, instead of down! And there she was, nearly at the edge of the wood, sitting on a branch just above Alice's head. Alice thought she'd be frightened, but she wasn't. She said she was looking for her Mum!" Duncan glared at Des at this point. He knew how guilty Gwen felt about abandoning Lily, and sure enough, two tears were rolling silently down her nose. Des looked at her and hurriedly changed the direction of his story.

"But actually I think she just wanted an adventure. She rode back to the castle with Alice and Ollie, and enjoyed all the fuss! She was fine. She's quite a character, that wee dragon of yours. She seems to have given young Georgie a few ideas!"

"Oh dear!" said Gwen

"There's one good thing about it – Angie will never want to see her again!" Duncan said again, trying for some comfort. "She may be rare and gold, but she's no longer the sweet baby Angie's always thought!"

"How are we going to keep her away from Katt?" asked Tom.

"Perhaps she'll persuade the wretched creature to leave!" said his father, but stopped under the furious glare of his wife and children. "Well, it is a problem, you have to admit," he added, defensively. "Where's Des going to sleep, if Tom's moved into the Bone Cave?"

"I'll be fine out here by the fire," Des said, yawning widely. "Time I got back to roughing it. I've got soft staying in that place of Angie's. I think I'll give the cat a wide berth, though. She seems to have taken against Duncan and me."

During the next three weeks, life settled down. The weather warmed, though the nights were still chilly. There were plenty of heavy showers, but no solid days of rain and low cloud, which were so depressing, and when the sun shone the young dragons began to feel that summer was almost beginning. Emily kept a secret daily watch for the return of Alice and the others, but so far there was no sign of them. She also spent time thinking about her Gran, and trying hard to pick up any mysterious Call which would tell her that it was time to leave for Wales with Des.

The day after his arrival with Lily, Des had joined Emily on the top of Ben's head and told her, in a low voice, the full story of Lily's escape, and how she had been found and rescued by Lisa and Megan. "Those young friends of yours were pretty good," he admitted. "Their dogs found her on a tree branch, like I said, and she took a liking to young Megan and let her carry her home. Alice said Megan wanted to keep her for a bit, but fortunately Lisa persuaded her that wasn't safe and they both set out to find you or Alice."

"The parents didn't find out, did they?" Emily said, rather horrified by Lily's narrow escape.

"Fortunately, no. Alice and Ollie kept quiet, obviously. They just pretended they'd found her themselves and carried her home. Even Ollie's changed his mind about trusting those Humans! Alice made Lily promise to keep quiet. She forgot of course, and chatted to Georgie about 'her friend Megan', but everyone assumed she was making it all up and took no notice."

"Thank goodness we made friends with them when they first broke into the cellar," Emily said. "Anything might have happened if they hadn't rescued Lily."

Des chuckled at her smug expression. "All right, you win!" he said. "Alice said much the same when she told me the story! Shall we tell Tom?"

Emily considered. "No," she said. "He's sometimes careless. He let it out to Wattie and Lottie the other day. He's much too busy thinking about Katt."

After two days, Tom was allowed to creep into his cave to tell Katt about Lily. He wasn't allowed too near the kittens, but Katt listened and agreed not to attack Lily if she strayed into the cave. A regular supply of food that didn't require her to go hunting for herself obviously helped! Already the kittens seemed bigger and stronger, though still blind and helpless. Emily secretly thought that growing inside an egg and hatching as a fully formed miniature dragon was a much better start in life!

Swimming and fishing and Tail-Stane kept Tom from bothering Katt and her kittens too often, and when Des was part of any trip to the loch and the otters, Emily usually decided to go too. Des taught her to land on water without getting wet wings and how to float gently, paddling her legs and keeping her head and wings held high. He said it was a useful Travellers' trick that he'd learned from his Bonxie friend, and made her practise it, especially when wind ruffled the loch into waves. At other times, she and Des made trips to the tree house and the camp site by the smaller loch, making repairs, clearing invading brambles and checking for intruders. All was ready for the return of the English family, but still they didn't appear.

"They'll come!" said Des when Emily complained. This morning they were taking a longer flight up the mountain, so Emily could show him the new cave that she and her mother had found. "It's still pretty cold at night, and they might be waiting for Old George to decide what to do. Ange keeps nagging him to stay with her, but I get the feeling he doesn't really want to." He was quite impressed with the cave, and pointed out that he might use it himself as emergency shelter if there was a long run of wet weather while Katt was still occupying Tom's cave. The ravens, who had finished building their nest, flew round their heads screeching in complaint at the intrusion, so Emily and Des left and flew to the top of the hill to gaze south and think about all their absent friends.

"I wonder how Gran is," Emily said after a long silence. She thought a lot about her, but seldom spoke in case she started to cry. If it was just Des it didn't matter, she decided. Des put a comforting wing round her.

"She'll be getting weaker, but making the most of her time. Gazing out to sea from her cave, chatting to the seabirds, enjoying the sunshine; talking to your Gramps and helping him to make his plans, and thinking about all of you. Do you pick up her feelings? I don't mean a Call, just a sense of how she is?"

"I think she's sort of happy," said Emily, thoughtfully.

"I think you're probably right. As soon as her Call comes, we'll go, I promise. Come on, let's give your wings some more training. Race you home!"

## Chapter 18

# Wild Kittens

Three days later, as they were finishing breakfast, a small striped kitten wobbled out of the cave, blinking in the light. Lily was the first to spot it and leapt up with a cry of delight, but her mother caught her before she could rush across and knock it over. Before anyone else could move, Katt shot out of the cave, glared round at the assembled dragons, hissed a warning, picked up the kitten by the scruff of its neck, and carried it back inside.

"That's the thanks you get!" said Duncan to his wife, but everyone ignored him.

"That's Archie," said Tom, sounding as proud as though the kitten belonged to him. "I thought he'd be the first to come out. His eyes opened first, and he's been exploring my room. He likes playing with bits of bracken and the end of my tail if I twitch it for him."

"What did you say his name was?" Emily asked, rather jealously.

"Well, I call him Archie. His mum just calls them all Kitt, with that kind of spitting sound she makes, but I decided they needed proper names. The other ones are Stripes and Mags. I called her after Maggie."

Duncan looked at Tom and shook his head sadly.

"Le' go!" said Lily crossly to her mum, lashing her tail, but Gwen refused.

"When all the kittens come out, and are a bit bigger and less wobbly, you might be able to play with them," Gwen said to her squirming daughter. "But only if Katt says you can! Are you listening, Lily?"

"No!"

"Even kittens can scratch and bite, so you'd better be careful!" Duncan was still trying to put his point across.

"I'll talk to Katt and tell Lily when it's safe," Tom assured them. Duncan rolled his eyes and sighed heavily in mock despair, and Des grinned and took pity on him.

"If this lot want to mess around with kittens, why don't we go off for the day? A hunting trip! Didn't you say there were plenty of grouse further up? I haven't had roast grouse for ages."

"Excellent idea, mate!" said Duncan. "Let's escape from these cat-worshippers!" Tom, who had been about to plead to be allowed to join the hunting trip, decided it would be a waste of time.

"You could bring some eggs, if you see any," Gwen added, "though only one from each nest, remember! And look for beetles. It's ages since we had a good broth." She went inside to find a bag.

A few minutes later, Duncan and Des flew off, disappeared behind the looming shape of Ben McIlwhinnie, and were absent for the rest of the day. During the next few days they took more long flights away, and usually came back with some good food for the pot, including new varieties of beetle and some rather strange mushrooms. Meanwhile, Katt found it more and more difficult to keep her family from wandering into all corners of the cave, and the dragons had to step carefully to avoid falling over them. Emily was delighted to find them sleeping in her bed one afternoon, and annoyed Tom by gloating about it.

The three kittens emerged properly two days later, and were allowed to play outside the cave, under the watchful eye of their mother, who settled herself on Ben's boot and stretched out in the sun. Lily, warned not to be too rough, was allowed to play with them, but it was soon obvious to everybody that the kittens were well able to look after themselves. Katt relaxed, and only became hostile when Duncan was around. She was suspicious of Des until her kittens used him as a climbing frame one afternoon, while he was having a nap. They hauled themselves slowly up the ridge of his spikes, Archie reaching the one on the top of his head first, and leaning down to bat at Mags and Stripes coming after him. As Des only opened one eye sleepily and didn't seem to mind, even when Archie slipped and hung on perilously by one claw, Katt relaxed and rolled over in the sun, leaving them to it.

To Tom's disappointment, Lily was the kittens' favourite, and the four of them spent many hours tumbling, chasing each other and mock fighting. But they would crouch in ambush and leap out on anyone who was passing, so Emily and Tom were just as likely to be their victims. When they were exhausted, they often curled up beside any dragon who happened to be sitting down, though once, when they chose Duncan, Katt immediately jumped down, picked them up one by one and removed them to the safety of the inner cave. She kept up a fierce growl through a mouthful of kitten as she did so. It was obvious that Duncan would never be forgiven for his earlier attempt to get rid of her. Emily felt quite sorry for him; after all, she thought, it was her father who had sternly vetoed Tom's idea of taking the kittens for a fly.

"Des gave the otters rides when they were wee!" he had protested.

"Only over the loch! They were perfectly safe falling into the water. What do you think would happen to those three if they fell off?"

"I thought cats always fell on their feet!"

"Stop arguing, Tom, you CAN'T take them flying. Give them a gallop down the hill, if it makes you happy." So Tom did, and Emily galloped Lily to keep them company. Like Tom she was enjoying the kittens, but kept hoping that Alice would be in time to see them before they grew too big. She knew that it wouldn't be long before Katt took them away to teach them to hunt and look after themselves.

"Don't worry," said her mum. "That cat knows the value of all these babysitters! She'll not leave in a hurry." But even she was secretly wondering why their English friends had not travelled north as they had promised.

Very early one morning, Emily woke with a start. She had been dreaming, but the dream faded away as she realised with a jolt of excitement, that her Gran had come into her mind so strongly that it must surely be a Call. She closed her eyes and tried to hear a voice. What she heard were not words, but a strong sense of

Nan's feelings. Nan wanted her to come. Now! As soon as she could, before it was too late. Feeling breathless, she sent her message back. "I'm coming, Gran, I'm coming..." and rolled out of bed to look for her mother.

Sure enough, Gwen was coming out of her cave too. "Did you hear the Call?" Emily whispered, hoping the others wouldn't wake. Her mother nodded.

"Yes, I heard it too. You will be in time, don't worry. Don't wake the others yet. Let's go outside."

They tiptoed past Des, curled up and snoring gently, and flew together up to Ben's head to watch the sun rise. "Why didn't Des wake when the Call came?" Emily asked.

"He doesn't hear it. It's a rare gift, Emily. Few dragons have it. It can be a blessing but sometimes a curse. Why you and Nan and I have it is a mystery."

"Old George has it too."

Gwen smiled fondly. "Yes, he will have heard the Call from Nan. I wonder what he'll do. He's such a wise old dragon. I'm sure he'll know if it's safe for him to travel. You might even see him in Wales."

They fell silent, then Emily burst out, "Can't we wake Des? We ought to be going!"

"All in good time," her mother said calmly. "I have everything ready for you."

"I wish you could come too!" Emily said, feeling tears start in her eyes.

"I said my goodbyes to Nan, remember? She and Edward know that I can't leave Tom and Lily again. You are growing up, Emily. That's why Nan wants you."

"I don't feel very grown-up just this minute," Emily wailed, sniffing.

Gwen smiled and put a wing round her. "Those are grown-up tears," she said.

They sat in comfortable silence for several minutes, and then saw Des roll over and stretch. When he looked up and saw the two of them, he jumped to his feet, sleep forgotten. "Is it the Call?" he said.

"Yes," said Gwen. "We both heard it. It's time for you to go."

Des spread his wings and flew to join them on Ben's head. He smiled at Emily. "Ready for your big adventure?" he asked quietly.

"Yes!" said Emily. "Can we go right away?"

# Chapter 19

# Journey to Wales

It did not take them long to pack the essentials Des decided they would need for the journey, and almost before Emily had got used to the idea, she was bidding farewell, with hugs and a few tears, to all her family, gathered between Ben's boots. Just before they set off there was another surprise. Glancing up at Ben before she left, Emily had a shock when she realised that the huge eyes had opened, and Ben was smiling down at her.

"I believe you are off on a great adventure, young Emily," he said. "This is an important journey, but you must not be too sad at its end. I know why you are going. Winter is over, so you do not need my help on your travels this time. You have your own strong wings! It is spring, the earth is awakening; there is life beginning and life ending. Desmond, guide her safely to Wales."

"Oh Ben, I wish you'd woken earlier!" Emily cried. "There's such a lot I wanted to tell you."

"Wake me when you return and tell me then. I shall want to hear about your travels too. Take my greetings to those you go to see. Fly safely, young dragons!"

With Ben's words ringing in her ears, and a last farewell wave to her family, Emily spread her wings and took off with Desmond, heading south for Wales and her waiting grandparents. As she left she heard Tom shout, "We've got kittens, Ben. Look! Wildcats. They're pretty rare! We found them in our cave when we got back...." His voice faded in the distance as they flew, and she turned to Des, flying beside her. "He really wanted to come with us. I'm glad he's got Katt and the Kitts to comfort him."

"They'll be a lot bigger by the time we get back. If they get too big and fierce, Duncan might throw them out."

"Mum won't let him do that."

"Tom might decide to go with them! Katt might leave of her own accord, though, if the others turn up. Too many dragons for comfort."

"D'you think we might see Alice and the others on our way? We're flying south, aren't we? Perhaps we'll meet them. That would be lovely!"

"Not very likely, though. Their route is over to the east."

"I don't really want Alice to arrive and find I'm not there."

"When Gwen explains, she'll understand. I'm sure they'll come before too long. Can you keep up this steady pace? Let me know if you need to slow down. We're OK at this height just now, but we'll need to fly higher when we spot some Humans' places. I know where we need to avoid. We'll have to do quite a lot by night, but you won't mind that, will you?"

"No, I got used to flying in the dark on our way home. I'm a bit worried about the sea, though," Emily confessed.

"You'll be fine, now you've practised landing on water. And if it's too rough, we'll wait for calmer weather. I daren't take any risks with you. I'd never be forgiven!"

For a while they flew steadily, without speaking, over stretches of empty hills and moors. Once they flew over a line of Singing Strings, which made Emily shudder, remembering the dreadful night of the blizzard, but they were well above their height so were in no danger. Further on they passed above a real castle, with huge towers and walls still intact. She wished they could have gone down lower to explore, but soon it was out of sight, hidden behind a hill. "Aunt Angie would like to live in that one!" she murmured to Des, who grinned back cheerfully. "She'd call herself Princess Angelica!" he said.

A little later, Des decided it was time for a rest, and headed towards some thick bushes on the banks of a wide river. "I could go a bit further," Emily protested, but Des was firm.

"Rest before you really need it," he said. "Good rule of Travelling. Then you won't be caught out looking for a safe place when you're ready to fall out of the sky. Come on, this place looks safe enough." They spiralled down and landed close to the water. It was clear and cold, and gave them both a refreshing drink before they brought out a snack from the bag Des had carried. They were sheltered from the wind, and the sun was warm on their scales. Emily began to feel rather sleepy! Realising, Des gave her a nudge.

"Another stretch before you get a sleep," he said, and led the way out of the bushes to a place clear for a take-off. As they rose over the river, they both looked down, and, too late, realised that a solitary fisherman, standing in mid-stream, was staring at them in wide-eyed amazement. Des veered towards some trees that hid them from sight, and Emily followed closely.

"He saw us, that Human! What shall we do?" she asked breathlessly, but Des was laughing.

"Often happens! No problem. The fishing Humans aren't dangerous. They're always on their own, they don't have guns or those picture-makers, so when they tell people what they saw, nobody believes them!" Emily joined in his chorus, "Everybody knows dragons don't exist!"

They flew higher and soon settled into a steady rhythm. "Tell me some more rules of Travelling," Emily suggested after a while. "I know about floating and resting and riding the wind, and how to tell the direction of flight by the sun, of course. What else is important?"

"Keep a good eye out for animals you can see on the ground," Des said. "You know about deer, of course, and they're in the wild parts. Sheep often are too, but if you see cows, that means you're near Human places, and you'll be better flying higher. Wee shaggy ponies are sometimes wild, but big shiny ones mean Humans too. As soon as you see the land broken up into squares with hedges and walls, that's Human, and you could be in danger of being spotted."

"What about the places where lots of Humans live? Villages and towns and things that I've read about? And trains and roads?

"Best avoided. Fly in the clouds if you can, or fly high. If it's a part of the land that's FULL of Humans, there's nothing for it but flying in the dark. Then you just get big patches of twinkly lights below you, but they're not dangerous. And you head for the dark bits if you have to land. I HAVE flown over huge patches of lights, with no decent landing grounds, but I wouldn't take you there – not 'til you're older. There's a very big one on the way to Wales, so that's why we have to head out to sea, to avoid it."

"What about flying machines? That one we saw in the snow was horrible!"

"We might see those later on. They're noisy, so you can hear them coming miles away and dodge. They go so fast they pass you in a minute. The important thing is not to panic. I once saw a very strange one, though," he added, more thoughtfully. "It was like a big round ball in the sky, bright red, and then it gave a huff of flame, just like a dragon. It was a long way away and moving with the wind. It must have been Human, not Dragon, but I couldn't see any of them. I've never seen another, but I'd like to, just in case there really *was* a dragon in there. You see some strange things, travelling!"

Emily was quiet for a while, thinking about all this. She realised that reading Human books was actually quite helpful in making sense of Travelling. When she said as much to Des, she was surprised that he agreed. "You're probably right. I never got round to learning myself. Perhaps the next best thing would be a Travelling Mate who can!" He grinned cheerfully at her, and she felt herself blushing with pleasure.

"I thought you were going to be travelling with Ollie. That's what he told us, anyway."

"He tried to talk me into it. I'll probably take him sometime, but I might make him learn to read first! Now, look ahead, and tell me what you can see."

"Lots of sheep, all together. And squares! And that's a road with machines running on it. Oh, are we coming nearer Humans?"

"Correct. Sheep in a flock spell danger, especially if there's a dog chasing them along. And everything square is Human. So what do we do?"

"Fly higher."

"Right again! Up we go. In a while we'll come to a big forest, and that's where we can camp out and sleep. Then we need to travel at night for a while."

Emily was amazed at his memory of the land below them, especially when the forest appeared exactly as promised, and she was led steeply downwards into a clearing with a stream running through it. After a meal, they both slept as the sun set and dusk deepened around them.

There was a good deal of the night left when Des woke Emily and they set off again. There were more clusters of lights below them now, and Des set a good pace, intending to leave this Human stretch of the journey behind before resting for the day in wilder parts. He hoped Emily could manage a long flight, but he needn't have worried. She gradually became less chatty as the night wore on, and the pace slowed a little, but she kept going without complaint, fascinated by the changing patterns of light below her and amazed at the thought of the hordes of Humans who must live there.

As a cloudy morning dawned, the Human lights were left behind and empty hills and moors stretched ahead. Realising that Emily really was very weary, Des led her down to a tumble of rocks on the moorland below; they could creep between them to hide, eat and sleep.

"Are we near the sea yet?" she asked, through a mouthful of cold roast rook from Des's stocks.

"Not too far. But it's not the Welsh sea yet. We'll sleep a while here, then go on over this stretch of moor towards the sea. It should be safe in daylight, especially if the cloud hangs around. You sleep and I'll keep watch." Emily closed her eyes thankfully.

She woke with a start some time later. Des was lying beside her, staring through a gap between the rocks. "Don't move!" he whispered, as he felt her wake up.

"What is it?"

"Humans. A line of them, walking, over there, see? Don't want to be spotted by them. They're the kind that might have those spy-glass things and picture machines. The danger is dogs, but there aren't any loose with that lot, fortunately. They don't seem to be heading this way, so we should be OK if we keep hidden until they disappear. Feeling better?"

"Yes lots better! Have *you* been to sleep?"

"No, thought it better to keep an eye out for trouble. Doesn't matter. I can go a long time without much sleep. Keep behind the rock, and I'll show you where we go next."

With one claw, he scratched some lines in the loose sandy soil. "We get to the sea at the end of our next flight. Then there's a shortish crossing to a big island in the middle of the sea. Not a deserted island, unfortunately. There are masses of Humans there, but I know a place in the middle where we can hide out for the day. After that it's the long sea crossing. But by then you'll be used to it, so you'll be fine." Emily gulped, and tried to feel as certain as he sounded.

The line of Humans disappeared over the brow of the hill, and Des relaxed. "Sun's dipping; we'll have a snack then start off. If we start a bit before dark, we should reach the sea by dawn. I know a good cave."

## Chapter 20

# Nan's Gift

The rest of that long journey passed in a blur for Emily. She decided that crossing the sea was rather boring, though recognising Human ships below her was quite exciting. She enjoyed exchanging chatty comments with seabirds, though was disappointed not to meet one of the famous Bonxies. The day on the big island was uncomfortable and rather frightening. There was not enough woodland cover for them to hide safely, and the number of flying machines that passed low overhead made her nervous during her spell on watch while Des slept.

After that, they flew out of sight of land, which was worrying, and had to resort to 'having a float', as Des called it, when their wings needed a rest. Fortunately the sea was reasonably calm, and Emily soon got used to the up and down motion of the waves. She thought how much Tom, such a good Water Dragon, would enjoy it. As they flew on in the dark, Des pointed to a line of lights ahead.

"That's Wales!" he said. "Not *our* Wales yet, but we're getting there. Another rest past those lights, and we'll push on through the hills and over the bay to Nan and Edward's cave. As soon as we land, I'll try a Huff. You've flown amazingly well, Emily!" Emily felt as though she would burst with pride.

Edward answered their Huff, assured them that Nan was awake and looking forward to seeing Emily, and told them to rest in a safe place before the last flight. But both Des and Emily were anxious to arrive, and they pushed on without too long a delay. This flight was over the sea, but within sight of the shore. Finally they flew over a finger of land sticking out to sea, backed by high snow-tipped mountains, wheeled round and headed for a line of rocky cliffs. Des pointed, and in the distance Emily could see a small figure with waving wings. He was on a ledge half way up a sheer cliff face, and lit by the light of the sinking sun.

As they flew closer and lower, Emily saw her grandad turn to call into the mouth of the cave behind him, and a moment later, a frail dragon appeared. Emily gasped "Gran!" and flew straight onto the ledge and into the hug that was waiting for her.

Nan felt smaller than she remembered, thinner, more fragile, her green colour paler with a tinge of grey. But her eyes were bright as she looked at Emily. "You have grown!" she said, leaning back to look at Emily. "What a beautiful young dragon you have become. And so brave, to come all this way!"

"I had Des to look after me!" Emily protested, blushing, and Nan stretched out a talon to Des. "Thank you, Desmond!" she said simply. Then she turned Emily to face the sea and sat on the ledge with one wing round her granddaughter. "Take Desmond to collect eggs for supper," she said to Edward.

"Only one from each nest, remember!" Emily called cheekily, quoting her mother, and Des turned with a talon gesture that she had a feeling was rather rude! She and Nan sat quietly staring over the sea, as the sun gradually reddened and disappeared.

"Remember the sunset over the sea in Scotland?" said Nan quietly. "When I said you would soon be visiting me in Wales? And now you have."

"I didn't think it would be so soon," said Emily, with a trace of a sob.

"And you didn't think it would be to say goodbye to me. I know. Neither did I. And I didn't think you would grow up quite so fast! I have heard about your adventures over the winter from your mother."

Emily hesitated for a moment, then made up her mind. "Not all of them," she said. "This is a big secret, Gran..."

"Of course it is! Whisper!"

So Emily, sitting close and speaking softly, told the story of the four children who had invaded their winter hideout, the stories they had told and gifts they had given, and how she and Ollie had seen a School Bus. She showed the pink bobble round her arm and relayed the story of Lily's rescue that Des had told her. As she finished and looked at her grandmother, wondering if she would be shocked, she saw Nan was smiling.

"Long ago I met a Human girl," she said. "She was called Catherine, and she loved to roam the hills. She had wild black hair and rode a grey pony..." Her voice trailed away as she remembered her long-lost youth. "I know that Duncan is very wary of Humans, Emily, but not all of them are dangerous, as you have found out for yourself. I think perhaps it is time for Dragons and Humans to move a little closer, but this will be a task for you not me! You say Desmond knows about your children?"

"Yes, he met them. He huffed fire and frightened them! But he's the only grown-up who knows."

Nan laughed. "Desmond is not a grown-up inside! Here they come. Over supper you can tell us about the family and your journey. We won't mention Humans!"

Nan ate very little supper, but Des and Emily made up for that, and told the old dragons about family life back at Ben McIlwhinnie's cave; how well Duncan's wing had mended; the return of the Otters; Tom's wildcat family; Lily's journey home with Des and her new bolshiness, which made them laugh.

"She is a strong character, that little golden dragon of ours!" said Edward, proudly.

Then Emily spoke of their journey, and talked on and on, telling of Travellers' Rules, the Fishing Human, the noisy island, the Human lights and the sea crossing in such detail that Des fell silent and let her talk, amazed at how quickly she learnt and enjoying her obvious excitement.

"I think you are already a Traveller!" said Edward finally, and Nan agreed. Des beamed with satisfaction and Emily blushed again. "But there is plenty of time to see the world, Emily. Enjoy your friends and your family and Ben McIlwhinnie's Glen for a little longer before you set off on your travels. Don't let Des hurry you."

"Me???" said Des, with his best expression of innocence, and everybody laughed.

"I must rest now. Come with me, Emily," Nan said, and led the way slowly through the narrow cave entrance, which twisted into the cliff and finally opened into a bigger chamber. To Emily's surprise, a small fire was burning, and the smoke was escaping through a crack high in the roof. Nan sat down with a sigh on a deep bed of bracken and took from round her neck the silver pendant on a fine chain that she always wore.

"This was given to me by Catherine," she said. "I am giving it to you."

"Shouldn't Mum have it?" said Emily, staring at the treasure with round eyes.

"No, it is yours. Gwen agrees. The real reason is that it is a Human token, and I have a feeling that in the future you will bring about an understanding between the few Dragons that remain and the Humans who will cherish them. Wear it always. It may last longer than your pretty bobble!" She placed the chain carefully over Emily's spikes and smiled in admiration.

"Beautiful!" she said with satisfaction. "Goodnight, Emily, my love."

Emily threw her wings round her Gran and gave her a loving huff. "Thank you Gran! It's my very greatest treasure. I'll remember all you've said about the Humans. It can be my new Quest! Sleep well. I'll see you in the morning." At the chamber entrance she turned and blew another huff and Nan blew one back before sinking onto her bed to sleep.

Edward met her as she turned the corner. "There's a bed for you," he said, pointing. "Des is fast asleep already over there! Sleep as long as you can – you've travelled a long way. I'll sit a while with Nan."

Emily snuggled down, not sure whether she was happy or sad. She thought she should be sad, but Gran was so calm and seemed so happy herself that Emily was thoroughly confused. Fortunately the exhaustion after their journey made her fall, like Des, into a long and deep sleep.

Neither of them woke when Edward came through the cave some hours later, sadly carrying a burden out into the dim light of a very early morning.

# Chapter 21

# The Grandparents' Farewell

Emily woke much later, bleary-eyed and confused. The cave was empty. For a moment she couldn't remember where she was. Then she came to herself with a rush, got up and tiptoed into Nan's room. The bed was empty. She began to panic, then thought Gran might have been feeling better and was up and having breakfast. She turned to dash outside and ran straight into Edward, who was coming to see if she was awake. She felt his wings close around her, and knew at once what had happened.

"Oh, Grandad!" she sobbed.

"She died very peacefully, still smiling, early this morning. I sat with her all night. She said that now she had seen you once more, spoken to you and passed on her gift it was time to go. She sent messages to everyone, but they can wait. Come outside with me."

Des was sitting on the ledge, gazing out to sea. He looked red-eyed and sad and put a wing round her. "I'm so sorry, Em! But we were in time to say good-bye. Be brave like Edward."

"Have a drink before we go down," said Edward practically, bringing hot mint tea.

"Down where?" asked Emily, sniffing back her tears and trying to be brave.

"You'll see!" said Des.

A few minutes later, Edward launched himself off the ledge and led them round the cliff and down to a hidden cove. As they flew down to a tiny sandy beach, marked by the retreating tide, two dragons came from behind the rocks and watched them land. Emily stared, open-mouthed.

"George! And Ollie! How did *you* know?"

"Like you, I got Nan's Call," Old George said. "I decided to come and say goodbye. Ellen insisted that I could not come alone, so Ollie came to look after me." He smiled fondly at his grandson, who looked a bit embarrassed, Emily thought, as she hugged George.

"Are the others still at the Castle?" she asked.

"They are on their way to your glen," George answered. "That is why Oliver didn't come with me. He wanted to take Ellen and the children north in safety. I think you will find them waiting for you when you get home."

"It's time," said Edward quietly, and Emily saw that the sun had risen above the mountains behind them and was shining in a broad path out across the bay.

Between them, Des and Ollie dragged a broad wooden raft across the sand to the water's edge, and Emily saw the body of her Gran lying on it, wings folded by her sides, tail curled and head turned as if asleep. She thought of her mother far away, and sent the picture in as strong a Call as she could manage. Then she walked between the two old dragons, and all five waded into the water together, pushing the raft until it floated free. George stopped and the four stood and allowed Edward to carry on alone. Suddenly he gave a mighty Huff, and a jet of flame burst onto the raft. Des stepped forward, and together they pushed the flaming raft into deeper water, and allowed the tide to take it out to sea.

As the five dragons stood together in silence on the wet sand, watching the fiery raft grow smaller in the distance, there was another sound; the sound of a huff even louder than Edward's, coming from above. Rising into the air over the clifftop, floated a huge red balloon, travelling directly along the sun's path and following Nan's funeral bier as it headed out to sea. The dragons gazed in astonishment as three Humans leaned over the basket hanging below the balloon and pointed down at them.

"Humans! Better hide!" Ollie shouted, and caught Emily's hand to pull her towards the rocks. But George and Edward stood firm.

"NO! We will not run and hide. We will face them proudly and wave a greeting!"

The five dragons stood tall and waved their wings at the Humans above them. The balloon drifted lower until it was almost directly above the burning bier. Then with a whoosh of flame it began to rise and the dragons saw three arms waving back and heard a call over the water. The balloon slowly dwindled into the distant sky, and at the same time, Nan's burning raft sank beneath the waves.

The five dragons watched in silence.

"What if they try to find us?" asked Ollie finally, in a whisper.

George smiled. "We will no longer be here! And somehow I think that Humans who fly so quietly with Dragon's Breath are not a threat to us."

"Nan would have said so," said Edward. "It was a fitting farewell." Silently, Emily stared after the balloon with shining eyes, and the wind dried her tears.

Finally they turned their backs on the sea, and Emily realised that a small fire was burning among the rocks. She smelt roasting rabbit. "Is it a farewell feast for Gran?" she asked, and Edward nodded. "A farewell feast for us all!" he said. "Let's enjoy it!"

"Ollie caught the rabbits this morning," said George proudly. "Good thing I brought him! Rabbits run too fast for me these days!"

They sat round the fire and while the rabbits charred black enough for dragons, Edward flourished a flagon. "The very best Old Firewater!" he said, and handed it to Des to pass around. Des served George and Edward and then hesitated at Ollie, who was looking hopeful.

"I think he's old enough, don't you?" he said to George, who nodded.

"I think he has proved that he is. But better, perhaps, not to tell his mother!"

Ollie beamed, accepted a mug and took a large mouthful. Next moment he was choking and spluttering, his eyes streaming.

Des grinned. "I was about to say take a small sip," he said, patting Ollie on the back. "How about you, Emily?"

"No thanks!" said Emily. "I'll stick to water." But she was pleased when Edward presented her with ginger fizz instead.

When Ollie had stopped coughing, gulped some water and promised to drink the rest of his Firewater more carefully, George raised a toast. "To Nan. May her wisdom live on!" They echoed his words and drank.

"And to the younger generation," Edward added. "To the three of you, with Alice and Tom, Georgie and Lily. Live long and keep the memory alive."

Emily clutched her pendant tightly in one talon. "We will!" she promised.

"Of course we will!" said Des cheerfully. "That rabbit looks black enough. Let's eat, and then I think we'd better make plans for heading back to Scotland. I know you trust those flying Humans, but we don't want to attract too much attention." He broke the rabbits into chunks and handed them round. For a few minutes, everyone munched hungrily without speaking.

It was Edward who broke the sound of crunching bones.

"I'm not coming to Scotland with you," he said. "I want to tell you of a long cherished plan that Nan and I agreed. You know that I have Irish blood; the gold on my spikes tells you that. For several months now, Nan has received Calls from dragons in Ireland, wanting to make contact with others, to create a community instead of scattered wanderers and settlers as we have become. There are a good many of them there, it appears. We agreed that after her death I should fly over and make contact. My last Quest! Emily, I know that Gwen and Duncan wanted me to live out my days with the family in your glen, but this is my decision. I hope you will explain so that they understand."

Emily looked downcast, but promised to do her best. She was disappointed, but excited at the thought of a colony of dragons in Ireland. "Grandad," she said. "Lily is gold all over! Don't tell the Irish dragons, will you? They might want to steal her."

"Certainly I will tell them about Lily!" Edward said. "She might be important. But I'll make sure nobody comes to take her away."

"Whatever you do, don't let her think she's important!" Ollie broke in. "She's quite bad enough without any encouragement."

"Yes, keep it a dead secret," Des agreed, remembering past battles with the determined little dragon. "We'll let you know when we want her taken away!" Emily smiled, feeling reassured on that point, but she was still a little worried.

"Will you be all right going all that way alone, Grandad?"

"I shall have a companion."

"I'm going with Edward," said Old George quietly. "I am fit and well now, thanks to Ellen and Maggie and like Edward I feel the need of one last Quest. I will take greetings from an English dragon to join the Scots and Welsh messages, and we will see what we can do in the time left to us."

The three young dragons stared at their elders, amazed. Des broke the silence. "I ought to go with you to help..." he began.

"But you have promised to take Emily home. And Ollie must go back with you to join his family. They still have a little growing-up to do! As for you, Desmond, you must make your own decisions after you have delivered them safely. But I think you have learnt the value of a home though you remain a Traveller at heart."

"Jump out the fire, Ollie," said George. "There is work to do before we all set off. Let's head back to your cave. Lead the way, Desmond."

For the rest of the day they busied themselves, clearing the cave of all traces of Dragon and collecting and packing supplies for five travellers. Edward gave Emily Nan's last messages for her family then, as the sun was setting, he and George made ready to depart. Emily knew she would not see them again, but she was a little cheered by George's parting words. "Remember the Call, Emily! Keep up your practice, and I will send you news."

The two old dragons rose into the sky and set off for the West as the sky deepened to the gloaming, and the others waved in farewell.

"I hope they'll get there OK," said Ollie. "Is it very far?"

"Not too far over the sea," Des answered. "They'll probably reach Ireland by morning. After that, who knows? They will have to trust the Call. Come on, we need to get going ourselves. Our journey is much longer. Let's make the most of the night!"

Three Humans with binoculars lay flat on the clifftop and watched the last of the dragons fly up from the ledge and head towards the north.

"The same five. Two going due west, and two north. Definitely dragons – small ones, different colours. Amazing! Pity we're too far for a decent picture."

"No it isn't," said the second. "We know what we've seen. No point telling anybody, they'll think we're making it up. Everyone knows dragons don't exist."

"Shall we look for some more?" This was the youngest, an eager teenager.

"No. When we saw them on the beach they seemed almost human. I think they were cremating a dead dragon with some sort of ceremony. And they waved. We may see them again, we may not. But we won't go looking. They've gone. Good luck to them!"

## Chapter 22

# Homecoming

By the time she, Des and Ollie reached the bottom of their glen in an early dawn, Emily felt like a fully-fledged Traveller. Des had listened in amusement as she and Ollie vied with each other over their knowledge of the Travellers' Rules and the comparative speed and strength of their wings. Ollie was still determined to become Des's travelling mate, but he was gradually realising that he had a rival! The three kept up a companionable banter through long night flights, and Ollie told about his family's preparations for a summer in the Scottish glen, and how sad Maggie and Harold were to see them go.

"Though I know Ange was glad to be rid of us," he finished. "But Des, she's convinced you'll be flying back there as soon as you've 'sorted them out', as she says." Des shuddered in mid-air. "No, it's a summer of freedom for me!" he declared.

"Did they know that George was planning to go away?" Emily asked. "Won't they be expecting him to come back with us?"

"I don't think anybody knew. It was a surprise to me!"

"I'll miss him," said Emily. "But it'll be lovely to see Alice! Oh look! Look! There's Ben!"

"Where?" said Ollie.

Emily pointed ahead to where the distinctive shape could be seen in the distance. "Oh, I do hope he's awake! I can't wait to tell him all the news!"Tired though she was, she increased her speed a little and the others followed. In a little while the loch came into sight, and Emily swooped lower as a bright blue figure splashed onto a rock, waving wildly and scattering drops. Seconds later the young otters appeared as well, but by then Tom was furiously shaking his wings dry before speeding after the three travellers.

Emily was bursting with pride as she led the way down to the familiar fireplace between Ben McIllwhinnie's boots, and rushed to hug her parents. Ollie and Des landed side by side on the right boot and watched the greeting. Tom caught up and joined Lily, both of them dancing with excitement.

"But where are George and Edward?" Duncan asked finally, when he had greeted Ollie and Des as well. "Nothing's happened to them, has it?"

"Wherever they are, they are well," Gwen said. "I know that much, but we need you three to supply the details. Ollie, I think you should fly on to your camp. You'll find the family waiting for you, and you can tell them all the news. You're not too exhausted for the last mile are you?"

"I really want to see Alice!" Emily protested as she waved Ollie away, but her mother was firm.

"Bed for you! There'll be plenty of time for us to hear all about your adventures when you've had a decent sleep."

Even the thought of her bed made Emily feel sleepy. "All riiightt!" she said through a huge yawn. "Des, you can tell them where the Gramps have gone, but nothing else. Promise?"

"Promise! I'll leave the telling to you. I'm for bed myself. Is the cave still full of cats?"

"Katt's taken them out for hunting practice," said Tom. "The kittens are quite big now....." he was all set to elaborate, but Duncan interrupted. "You can have the Bone Cave, Des. But first, where on earth are George and Edward?"

Emily didn't wait to hear Des's explanation. She crawled into the cave, fell onto her new-made bed and was almost instantly asleep.

It was late afternoon when she woke, and Gwen, hearing her stirring, brought mint tea and sat down on her bed for a private talk.

"I knew when Nan died," she said. "It was the middle of the night, but I felt the Call. And the next morning I saw her, lying as if asleep by the edge of the sea. Was that you?" Emily nodded and her mother smiled. "You certainly have the gift! Were you in time for a last talk with her?" Emily nodded again, feeling too close to tears to speak. "Good. That will have made her last day very happy."

"She gave me her pendant and a Quest," Emily whispered.

"I know. Don't tell me about it. You need to think it out for yourself. There's plenty of time. Nan didn't want you to grow up too fast. Des has told us where Edward and George have gone, and why. I'm not really surprised. They might be old, but neither of them will want to sit around idly, just getting older! George will send a Call when he has some news for us. Why don't you get up and fly down for a dip in the loch before supper? Des is already there, with Tom."

Emily found her father starting to prepare supper outside. She gave him a hug. "I LOVED travelling, but it's nice to be home. I'm going down to the loch."

"Good. Have a wash. You're nearly as grubby as Des!" She gave him a friendly punch and set off.

The sun had warmed the shallow end of the loch, and she enjoyed her swim. When she climbed out, a good deal cleaner, Des and Tom surfaced and swam to join her. As they spread their wings in the sun, Emily turned to Tom. "Gran gave me a message for you," she said. Tom looked a little worried and glanced at Des. "It's all right. I'm not going to cry.

She sent her love to you, and said, 'Tell Tom he must never forget his Wildcat.'"

"Of course I won't, but what do you think she meant?" Tom looked from Emily to Des in bafflement.

"Don't try to work it out, just remember it," Des advised.

"Did she give you a message?"

"Yes."

"What was it?"

"It was for me," said Des firmly.

"She gave me a sort of Quest," said Emily, "but I don't know really understand it either."

"You will when the time is right." This was an unusually serious Desmond, and they both stared at him in surprise. He switched to his familiar cheerful grin. "Hope Duncan's got supper ready. I'm starving!"

Supper was grouse, chillie and nettle stew, so tongue-tingling and spicy that Emily hardly noticed that bulrush roots had been added, and in any case, was feeling too happy to complain. Katt and her kittens trotted past, obviously full after their hunt, and headed into the cave, Archie giving the end of Des's tail a playful swipe on the way. The kittens had certainly grown, Emily thought. Lily would miss her playmates when they left!

After they had eaten, Tom brought up the subject of Nan's message. "What do you think she meant?" he appealed to his mother, who just smiled knowingly and said he would need to work it out for himself.

"Oh, I nearly forgot!" cried Emily. "There was a message for Dad as well. Gran said, 'Tell Duncan, when the time comes, let them fly.'" There was a brief silence.

"Was that all?"

"Yes I think so. Love to everyone as well, of course."

"Hmm." Duncan made no further comment.

"What about Mum?" asked Tom.

"I've been given my message already," said Gwen with a smile. "And I have a new picture from the Call! Two old dragons sitting round a fire with strangers, sharing food and talk."

"Oh great!" said Emily. "They got to Ireland safely and met up with Irish dragons! I'll miss them, but I bet they have a lovely time. When can I go and see Alice, Mum?"

"In about two minutes," said Des, pointing upwards, and flying towards them they saw Ellen, Oliver, Alice and Ollie, with Georgie riding on his father's back. Emily leapt to her feet and hugged Alice as soon as she landed. "I've SO much to tell you! Let's go up to Ben's head!" she said when the greetings were over, and the girls allowed Ollie and Tom to join them.

The four of them sat in a huddle, talking quietly. Ollie told Alice and Tom about the Humans in the red balloon, Nan's fiery bier and catching the rabbits for her farewell feast. He flashed a warning glance at Emily, who understood and *didn't* tell how he had choked on his Firewater! Instead she told them the secret of Nan's Human friend, and showed the pendant that was Catherine's gift. "And when Gran gave it to me, she said it was time Humans and dragons came closer," she finished, "and I said that would be my new Quest. But I don't really understand how I'm going to do it."

"Did you tell her about our friends? Lisa and the others?" Alice asked.

"Yes. She knew it was our secret. That's when she told me about her friend Catherine. What do you think I have to do? How can I start?"

There was a thoughtful silence. Tom looked from face to face, waiting for one of the others to speak. "I think we've already started, in a way," said Alice. "We made friends! Finn said they had never told anyone else about us. Lisa and Megan proved they could be trusted when they brought Lily back to us. I could see that Megan really loved her, and Lily wasn't frightened at all."

"So I decided to be friendly instead of frightening," Ollie added. "I trust them too – you girls were right. I don't think we need to do anything else just yet, Em. But when the time comes, we've made a start, as Alice said. After all, we know where they live! We can find them again. Ssh, someone's coming! Oh it's only Des!"

Des hovered above them. "Yes, only Des, and I didn't hear a thing! Your folks say it's time to go. They're planning a huge feast for tomorrow! And Gwen says it's bedtime, Tom. Your cats are already asleep, so don't make your usual row." Tom aimed a tail-swipe at him as he flew down with Alice and Ollie.

Des landed beside Emily. "So now you've told Alice and Tom, how about Ben? Shall we wake him?"

Emily beamed. "Yes, let's!" They leaned down together and huffed smoke past the giant's nose until the huge eyes opened and looked up.

"Ah! My two favourite dragons, Emily and Desmond, home from their travels! Please stop huffing, Desmond, you'll make me sneeze, and you know what that leads to! Sit on my hand, so I can listen without craning my neck." He raised his hand, and Des and Emily sat side by side. "That's better! Now, Emily, tell me all your news."

He listened carefully, nodding his head solemnly, as Emily, with occasional interruptions from Des, told the whole story. "And there's one last thing," she said. "I haven't told anyone, not even Des, and nobody else must know. George sent me a Call too. But in *my* picture of him and Edward round the fire with the stranger dragons, there was someone else. Two Humans, sharing their talk!"

"Ah!" said Ben. "So Nan's Quest has started."

"It's my Quest too! What am I supposed do, Ben?"

Ben smiled at her. "Have a lovely summer with your friends. Enjoy life with your family; play with the kittens, swim with the otters, help Tom and Lily with their growing-up. Look after my glen. Cherish your gift and practise the Call. And wait! Desmond, you too had a message from Nan. May I hear it?"

Emily turned to look at Des, in case he wanted her to go, but he answered without hesitation, looking up at Ben. "She said, 'Be in no hurry. Be patient until the time is right.' And I will. I promised her." He looked solemnly at Ben, and then turned to Emily, still staring at him, and grinned his old cheerful grin. "No worries!" he said.

Ben nodded his huge head. "A wise old dragon! I wish I had met her. Keep her in your thoughts and I too will listen for the Call. Good night, young dragons. Wake me for the Feast tomorrow, and dance your Dragon Reel again for me!" He closed his eyes.

"Goodnight, Ben!" A faint call came from below, and Emily turned to go. Dusk was falling. "Coming?" she asked, feeling suddenly unexpectedly shy.

219

Desmond smiled. "In a while. I want to watch the stars come out. The gloaming is a good time for dreaming! Sleep well."

"I think I'll dream too," said Emily, and performed a joyful loop round Ben McIlwhinnie's head before she headed home.

THE END

# Glossary

A short glossary of some of the Scots Language, as used by the young Otters in this book, the Bonxie in *Quest for Adventure* and some of the Hawks and Buzzards in *The Runaway* and *Dragons in Snow*

***Hint:*** *If you are puzzled by the spelling of a word, try reading it aloud as it is written. You will often guess what it means. Some of the words below are easy to guess, but some are more unusual and have special meanings.*

**Afore:** before

**Anither** : another

**Back th' noo :** back in a minute

**Bairns:** children

**Bidin':** living

**Birled:** whirled

**Blaeberries:** the Scots name for blueberries (or bilberries or whinberries in different parts of England)

**Bonxie :** Great Skua – a large fierce seabird

**Braw:** nice, good, lovely – general approval!

**Coorie doon:** snuggle up (or down)

**Daein':** doing

**Deid :** dead

**Dinnae:** don't

**Dinnae fash:** don't worry

**Dreich:** dark, drizzly, miserable weather (wonderful Scots word to describe a wet Highland day!)

**Drookit:** soaked with water, bedraggled (another good one!)

**Dugs :** dogs

**Feart:** frightened

**Frae:** from

**Gae:** go

**Geme:** game

**Gloaming:** evening, twilight or dusk (very important - the time of the Gloaming Huff)

**Guddle:** muddle

**Hae a shot**: have a go, try it

**Heid:** head, or chief

**Isnae:** isn't

**Keek:** look

**Ken:** know ('ye ken' is used exactly like 'you know')

**Loch:** a freshwater lake, like the one near the Dragons' cave (a little one is a 'lochan')

**Mair:** more

**Micht**: might

**Mingin'**: disgusting

**Nae:** No

**Naebdy:** nobody

**Nae danger:** no problem or no chance

**Neb:** nose

**Nicht:** night

**Onyways:** anyway

**Selkies:** seals (there are a lot of lovely old tales about Selkies told in Scotland)

**Ta'en:** taken

**Tatties:** potatoes – usually pronounced without the middle 't's

**Telt:** told

**Thirz:** there is or there are

**Wilnae:** won't

**Yez:** you – usually plural

**Yin:** one

**Yince:** once

# Acknowledgements

Special thanks to Peter this time, for putting up with all the cardboard boxes, as well as STILL keeping the old computer functioning, against the odds.

Kate, Rachel and Gill continue to find new readers and expand my school network; thanks to all the friends who keep their children, grandchildren, nephews and nieces supplied with dragons; thanks to Roddy, ace marketer; thanks to Simon at Kesley's Bookshop who has given support and encouragement from the beginning.

My grandchildren still keep up their enthusiasm for the project, and special thanks this time to David, our family wildlife expert, who first suggested that a Wildcat would be a good addition, and supplied names for the kittens and lots of ideas for that bit of the plot. Elise has been my most enthusiastic critic. Megan decided that dragons should visit Ireland, and memories of her in earlier life supplied ideas for bolshie Lily. (I was delighted when she recognised her former self.)

Thanks to Ali, who back at the beginning suggested a hot-air balloon – a difficult thing to fit into these tales so I hope he is pleased with its starring role; to Catherine, for inspiring Nan's Human Friend, to Finlay who lent his name; and to George, for the bulrushes.

Huge thanks as always, Caroline, and I hope you find many more opportunities to delight young readers with your lovely illustrations. Your painted cover-pictures adorn my walls – a lasting reminder of this series and the pleasure I have had in this writing project. It's been great working with you!

And my best love and thanks to Alison, who made it all happen, and recognised my mother Joyce in lovely Nan.

Finally, to my faithful readers, who may be sad that this is the last book, I bequeath my Dragons for you to carry the story on. Thank you!

# About the Author

Judy Hayman lives with her husband Peter on the edge of the Lammermuir Hills in East Lothian, Scotland, where there is a wonderful view and plenty of wildlife, but no dragons, as far as she knows. At various times in her past life she has taught English in a big comprehensive school; written plays, directed and occasionally acted for amateur theatre companies; been a Parliamentary candidate for both Westminster and the Scottish Parliament; and a Mum. Sometimes all at once. Now preventing the Lammermuirs from taking over her garden, being a Gran, writing Dragon Tales and visiting schools to talk about them takes up a lot of her time.

# About the illustrator

Caroline Wolfe Murray studied Archaeology at the University of Edinburgh and took a career path in the field, turning her hand to archaeological illustration. She has always had a passion for exploration and discovery which evolved from her experience of living in Spain, Belgium, Venezuela and New Zealand. She now resides in East Lothian with her husband James and her two young daughters Lily and Mabel, who have been her inspiration to work on a children's book.